ESCAPE
THROUGH THE
WILDERNESS

ESCAPE
THROUGH THE
WILDERNESS

GARY RODRIGUEZ

TATE PUBLISHING
AND ENTERPRISES, LLC

Published by Tate Publishing & Enterprises, LLC
127 E. Trade Center Terrace | Mustang, Oklahoma 73064 USA
1.888.361.9473 | www.tatepublishing.com

Tate Publishing is committed to excellence in the publishing industry. The company reflects the philosophy established by the founders, based on Psalm 68:11,
"The Lord gave the word and great was the company of those who published it."

Book design copyright © 2014 by Tate Publishing, LLC. All rights reserved.
Cover design by Hope Nixon
Interior design by Manolito Bastasa

Published in the United States of America

ISBN: 978-1-63268-201-7
Fiction / Action & Adventure
14.09.11

To Colette,
for so many reasons

CHAPTER ONE

Saturday, 8:14 p.m.

This is a KGX Channel 7 Breaking News Report. I'm Valerie Parker.

Four teenagers have gone missing tonight from an adventure camp in Northern Idaho. Early reports say the teens and their river guide were involved in a rafting accident sometime this afternoon. Their names are being withheld pending notification of their parents. Rescue teams are being assembled, according to local authorities. The camp earns the title, "The safest camp in Idaho" every year. Tragically, after today all that has changed forever. Stay tuned to KGX Channel 7 for more details as they develop…

ooooo

Thursday, two days earlier

It was a warm August afternoon and Camp Arrowhead buzzed with activity. New teen campers had been streaming in since mid-morning. Savannah Evans, who had arrived earlier in the day, was heading toward the message board to check out the day's schedule when she noticed another car pull into the drop zone.

Curious, she waited to catch a glimpse of the new camper. But before she saw the passenger, a huge commotion exploded in the arriving vehicle.

An agitated woman who appeared to be the girl's mother started yelling from inside of the car. "Come on, Jade! Hurry up and get out of the car; we've got a plane to catch!"

Savannah watched in shock as the distraught girl scurried out of the backseat as fast as she could. In tow were a backpack, two suitcases, and a purse slowly winding itself around the poor girl's arm. In an instant the auto sped off, leaving a trail of dust and the young teen in a heap. There were no hugs or even attempts at a good-bye, only a heartless door slam and the vehicle peeling off at a high rate of speed.

Staggering under the weight of her load, the devastated girl fell to the ground and began sobbing.

Savi was stunned by the dramatic scene happening in front of her.

What was THAT all about? Was that her mom? Savannah thought to herself.

Pretty rough no matter who it was!

She felt sorry for the distraught new arrival crying on the ground.

"How embarrassed I'd feel if that was me, especially with everybody watching." She thought.

"*I should go and help her.*"

She hurried over to the drop off area, bent down on one knee, and did her best to comfort the frazzled stranger.

"Can I help you with some of this stuff? It looks like a lot for one person to carry."

Startled, the girl at first tried to shake off the unwelcome intruder. "Leave me alone—I don't need any help," she said in a harsh tone. "Who are you, anyway?"

"My name's Savannah, but my friends call me Savi. I...I just thought you could use some help."

Savi waited patiently for the girl to collect herself. Slowly she lifted her tear-stained face to see who had spoken to her so kindly. The sight of her face made Savannah inhale sharply.

"What? I look stupid, right? I already know that." The girl said even more perturbed.

"No, not at all. I wasn't thinking anything like that. It's just...you're really pretty."

In her sixteen years of living in Oxford, Mississippi she never saw a girl as beautiful as this one. Despite the tear tracks on her face and a pair of puffy eyes, she looked like a real life sized china doll. Her milky white complexion contrasted by her long shiny black hair was stunning. When you added in her soft delicate features, she was flawless. As close to perfect as a girl her age could look.

The girl finally realized that Savi was only trying to be friendly and helpful.

"Thanks for saying that, Savi, but I don't feel very pretty right now...My name's Jade Chang—Sorry I snapped at you—Do you mind if I call you Savi?"

"Not at all, I'd like that," Savi replied with a smile.

"I feel like such a fool. I can't believe my mother did that to me," she said shaking her head.

"Well...you're not going to have to deal with her for a while. Come on. Let's go see what cabin you're in... Maybe we're in the same one."

Jade stood up and with Savi's help gathered up her belongings and headed for the camp office. As they walked, Savi looked down at Jade's Coach purse, Tumi suitcases, and North Face backpack. *All this great stuff... but she still seems so unhappy.*

During their walk to the office, Savi looked over at Jade and could see she was deep in thought and that her heart was heavy. So while carrying her suitcase with her right hand, she lifted her left and patted her gently on the back. Jade was touched by the kind gesture so she glanced over at Savi and gave her a friendly smile. Savi grinned back and felt hopeful that she might have already found a new friend at camp.

"Savi, I noticed you're limping. Did you hurt your ankle?"

"Actually, I hurt it a few years ago," she replied.

"Oh I didn't mean to..."

"That's okay, it's no big deal."

"No, really," Jade said apologetically, "I'm sorry for being so nosey."

"No worries," Savi replied. "It's not as if you asked me how much I weigh or something," as she rolled her eyes and gave Jade a friendly nudge with her elbow.

Both girls laughed and continued walking toward the camp office. On the way, Savi said to Jade, "How 'bout I tell you the story about my ankle later?" Then the two of them agreed to put off the subject for another time.

When they arrived at the office, they looked for the cabin assignments posted outside the door. Savi could tell Jade was already feeling a bit more comfortable and starting to relax.

"Jade over here…Those are the boys' cabins…Here's the girls'. I'm sure they'd be thrilled to see you, though," Savi joked.

Embarrassed, Jade threw her head back and then made her way over to where Savi was standing in front of the girls' cabin assignment board.

"You said, 'Chang,' right?" Savi asked, running her finger down the list of names.

"That's right," Jade replied.

"Here you are…Oh that stinks! We're in different cabins," Savi noted. "Want to go inside and see if they'll move us to the same one?"

Jade looked over at her and paused a moment… "Umm, okay. That sounds great."

The girls did their best to convince the camp director that they should be in the same cabin. Unfortunately, he wouldn't budge. But he told them he'd keep in mind their desire to be together when planning future events.

When they left the office, the girls decided to drop off Jade's stuff at her cabin and grab a cool drink. After leaving the snack shack, they found a shady spot on a carved log bench.

"I promised I'd tell you about my ankle. I guess this is as good a time as any."

"You know you don't have to," Jade replied.

"I know, but I want you to know how I got my limp."

"I have to admit...I am a bit curious."

"Well, when I was eight years old, the U.S. National Gymnastics Team came to Oxford, Mississippi to put on an exhibition at Ole Miss."

"Ole Miss?" questioned Jade.

"Oh sorry, that's short for University of Mississippi. Anyway, my dad took me to see the competition and that event changed my life."

Jade shrugged. "How?"

"Watching the different routines was so cool. I instantly fell in love with gymnastics, particularly the balance beam. The girls were so graceful but strong at the same time. I dreamed of becoming one of them. For the next three years I trained on the beam and competed in a bunch of events. My goal was to make the U.S. National Team."

Suddenly, Savi stopped. "I'm not boring you, am I?"

"No, not at all! I'm really interested. Keep going."

"In just three years, I was ranked fourth in the nation in my age category. Everybody was so proud of me. But only the top three girls went to nationals. The final cuts were a few years ago in Nashville. I was tied for second place with this girl named Julie, with only one routine to go—I was freaking out! I knew my only hope of beating her and advancing was to do a flawless routine and stick my landing. Everything was going great until my final element, an aerial summersault. It was always my most challenging move. I was hoping I could pull it off. The summersault was perfect but as I landed on the beam…" Savi paused and looked down at her ankle. "My left foot hit the beam wrong and my ankle snapped like a dry branch."

"Oh my gosh, that's awful! I'm so sorry."

"Yeah, me too. Because that ended my career in gymnastics and my dream of going to the Olympics."

"They couldn't fix it?" Jade asked.

"They tried, but it never healed quite right, so I've learned to live with it. I get around just fine, though."

"I can see that—Wow! That's quite a story. Thanks for telling it to me."

Well, now you know a little about me, but I know absolutely nothing about you. Next time we meet, it's your turn."

"That's a deal."

They both finished their drinks and stood up.

"I can't believe how tall you are! You must be at least 5'7"."

"Actually, I'm 5'8"," Jade said proudly.

"I knew you were up there. I've always been on the short side. Only 5'2". But you know what they say, 'good things come in small packages.'" Jade smiled and nodded in agreement. Then they said good-bye, and headed toward their separate cabins.

Savi called over her shoulder, "I'll look for you later!"

"Okay, later!" Jade yelled back.

Savi was on the way back to her cabin when she came upon three boys leaning against a big tree, joking around with each other. She caught one of the boy's eyes and he watched her as she walked by toward the cabins. He immediately noticed her limp and nudged his friends. "Look at that one. I didn't know this camp was open to special needs kids!" he said in a raised voice, most likely for her to hear. Again, the same boy blurted out, "I hope they don't match me up on some activity with 'lame girl.'"

Savi overheard the insult but pretended she didn't. She also heard one of the boys standing with him say, "Nice one, Conner!"

By the time Savi reached her cabin, she was red-faced and fuming. Alone, sitting on her bed, she stared out the window at Conner. She watched as he and his friends amused themselves at the expense of others walking by.

Here we go again, she thought to herself. *I thought I left those bullies back at school!* Then, she rose to her feet and stepped outside of the cabin. With an animated face and a loud voice she yelled in the bully's direction, "Hey, Conner! Your mom's on the phone and says you forgot to pack your blankie and Batman underwear!"

Instantly, a roar of laughter erupted from those within earshot of her clever retort. This time it was Conner's turn to feel the sting of humiliation. He slinked away to his cabin not to be seen again until the dinner bell.

Savi stood in front of her cabin triumphant, though she did feel somewhat ashamed for finding the taste of revenge so sweet. Suddenly, a familiar voice shouted from across the campground, "Savi, come look! We're paired up together for tomorrow's rafting trip! We're in the same raft!"

She leaped for joy and joined Jade at the message board for an energetic high five.

"And guess what? There are boys in our raft. Two of them!" Jade proclaimed excitedly. "One's named Rico Cruz and the other is some guy named Conner Swift."

"What?" Savi yelled. "Conner…I just met that jerk! I'm not getting in a raft with him. No way!" Savi vowed.

"Oh, yes you are, little lady!" Savi heard Camp Director Anderson say forcefully behind her. "All raft assignments are final. What's done is done. There will be NO changes!" the director reiterated as he walked away.

Savi stood staring blankly at the message board. *What could be worse than being in a raft with Conner Swift!* It wouldn't be long before she'd find out.

CHAPTER TWO

The lingering aroma of barbecued burgers mixed with the scent of pine trees and a crackling fire flavored the evening air as dusk gave way to a starlit night. The chirping of crickets added to the magical surroundings.

The bonfire was already casting a bright glow on the faces of those around it. Campers were beginning to circle the brick pit hoping to secure a warm spot and get close enough to hear the *Fright Night* stories about to begin.

Opening night of summer camp was renowned for the frightening tales told at the campfire. Girls brought blankets not only to bundle themselves up but to muffle their screams during the really scary stories.

"Jade, I'm over here!" Savi motioned. Jade spotted Savi and moments later the two sat next to one another on a big blanket. Across the way, Savi and Jade spotted Conner showing off his glitzy wristwatch to an interested onlooker.

"Who wears a watch anymore?" Jade asked in a mocking tone.

"I guess rich boys from Chicago's North Shore do," Savi replied.

"How do you know he's from Chicago?"

"I overheard some girls talking about him earlier today. Apparently his dad's a big shot and owns half the city. He's seventeen and seems to think he's God's gift to all the girls on Planet Earth!" Savi scoffed.

"I have to admit…I think he's kind of cute. But I'm put off by his cocky attitude and the nasty things he said to you earlier," she admitted.

"How'd you hear about that?" Savi asked.

"A girl in my cabin told me she overheard him taunting you this afternoon."

Unknown to the girls, Rico Cruz stood alone on the other side of the fire pit. He scanned the crowd of unfamiliar faces glowing in the firelight. Then he saw Jade for the first time, though he didn't actually know her name. The moment he saw her face, his heart skipped a beat, and he quit looking around. Her beauty surprised and infatuated him. He tried repeatedly to look away, but could not take his eyes off of her.

Are you kidding me? He thought to himself. *She's gorgeous!* Then he quickly looked around wondering if he had inadvertently said that out loud. He was relieved to find that his secret was safe for the moment.

Rico was already the "hot topic" with the girls throughout the camp. He was accustomed to lots of female attention, not only because of his good looks and dark complexion, but also because of his "bad boy" persona. He was known as one of those tough nice guys…the tender-warrior type.

All of a sudden, like dominoes falling one at a time, the crowd began to hush. A collective gasp soon followed the silence. Rico immediately looked over his shoulder to see a solitary hooded figure dressed in a black robe approaching the fire. When the mysterious stranger's face became visible in the firelight, several girls screamed. Everyone winced in fear at the hooded stranger's horrifying mask. Even Rico seemed a bit unnerved.

Jade and Savi were so scared that they covered their heads with the blanket. Now only their eyes were visible through a small slit in their covering. "I see now why they call it 'Fright Night'!" Savi said in a shaky voice.

Jade was too scared to talk.

Then the cloaked figure began to tell the first of his three scary tales. As the story unfolded, the tension level rose. Fear crept slowly over the spellbound campers like fog covering the stage at a rock concert. Hope for a good night's sleep abruptly vanished for most of the campers. Several teens were so terrified they actually sprang to their feet and scampered back to their cabins.

Meanwhile, the sinister figure stood quietly for what seemed like the longest time before he began another scary tale. But Jade decided she'd had enough and quickly tried to free herself from the blanket clutched tightly by Savi.

"Savi, let's run for your cabin!" Jade blurted out. "I don't care what anyone says, I'm not sleeping in some strange cabin alone tonight."

Before Savi could answer, the creepy storyteller started speaking again in his disturbingly deep and raspy voice.

"Before my last story, I am required to warn you about the disembodied spirits that lurk about at night here at Camp Arrowhead. They live to torment new campers, especially on 'Fright Night!'"

"Okay, we are for sure staying in the same cabin tonight!" Savi told Jade.

"Do you believe in spirits?" Jade asked nervously.

"Tonight, I do!" Savi responded, while pulling the blanket back over her head.

Again, the hooded man spoke and continued his final story. "For those of you who don't know, Camp Arrowhead is located just twenty-five miles from the legendary feeding grounds of a flesh-eating beast known as Vexel."

"OMG Savi, who the heck is Vexel?" Jade blurted out.

"I don't know, and I don't want to know!" Savi replied, her tone deadly serious.

Just then a girl yelled from the back of the crowd, "What does Vexel look like?"

The cloaked man pondered the question a moment and then replied, "Unfortunately, no one knows exactly what he is or what he looks like." After another pause, he went on to say, "Because nobody that has actually seen him has survived the encounter! There are also many rumors floating around about who or what it might be. Ten years ago there was an accident at a zoo about forty miles from here. Several dangerous animals escaped and were never found."

"What kind of animals?" another girl asked anxiously from the front row.

The hooded man turned toward her and answered slowly in his low and raspy voice, "A lion, a black panther, and a large gorilla. Many people believe that Vexel is one of those animals and now lurks and hunts in the nearby wilderness. Others think he may be a huge grizzly bear that survived a forest fire several years ago… but no one knows for sure."

All at once, Conner Swift jumped up and shouted confidently, "If I see Vexel, I'll kick his butt and eat him for lunch!" His boasting was greeted with a smattering of nervous laughter but mostly with mocking shouts of, "Yeah right, Conner!" and murmurs of doubt. Rico shook his head at Conner in disgust, and appeared instantly not to like him.

Conner continued to brag to those around him about carving up Vexel for lunch. Little did he know that by this time tomorrow, Vexel might be thinking the same thing about him!

CHAPTER THREE

Despite the warning the night before, no dismembered spirits were seen in Camp Arrowhead that evening. For many campers a fitful night's sleep had finally come to an end.

A golden sunrise ushered in the morning accompanied by a symphony of birds singing their favorite tunes. A poster by the message board displayed pictures of birds native to the region. Some of the proud members of the chirping choir were indigo buntings, northern cardinals, American gold finches, and song sparrows, just to name a few. The birds' beautiful and breathtaking harmony served as a pleasant wake up call for those still sleeping, including Savi and Jade.

Rico woke up at the crack of dawn because of his unfamiliar surroundings. He brushed his teeth and gave himself a quick shave. He then made his way across the camp to a huge grass field where others had assembled to play a football game before breakfast.

On his way to the field, he stopped at the message board to see his assignment for the rafting trip scheduled for later that day. To his great disappointment, he saw that he and Conner Swift were in the same raft. *Give me a break!* He thought. *How'd I end up with him?*

After getting over the initial shock, he noticed that two girls, Jade Chang and Savi Evans, were also slotted to be in the same raft. Although he had seen Jade the night before and had marveled at her beauty, he never got a chance to meet her or even find out her name. He didn't know it at the time, but today would be his lucky day!

In the meantime, Conner had heard about the early morning football game and was making his way to the field. A highly competitive person by nature, and in his estimation a superior athlete, he decided this might be a good opportunity to show off his ball handling skills.

When Conner arrived at the field, the kids were choosing up teams. Rico had been designated as a team captain based on his physique and strong arm that was hard not to notice during the warm-up that morning. Rico saw that Conner was looking for a team and he made sure it wouldn't be his. He intentionally skipped over Conner each time it was his turn to pick someone and was glad when they ended up on opposing sides.

Because of the limited number of participants, each of them had to play both offense and defense. When his team had the ball, Rico was quarterback. On defense, he lined up as a pass defender. On the other team, Conner was a receiver on offense and a pass rusher while on defense.

From the opening kickoff the boys were eager to impress each other with their athletic talents. But no one seemed more committed to shine than Conner.

"I'll be streaking down the right sideline, hit me deep," Conner petitioned his quarterback in the huddle.

"If you get open, I'll get you the ball," the QB replied.

The teams faced each other on the line of scrimmage ready for the first play. Rico stood on the other end of the line from Conner guarding a different receiver. "Hut-one, hut-two, go, go!" the quarterback yelled. As soon as the ball was snapped, Conner raced down the sideline, and as he had promised, the quarterback delivered a perfect strike into Conner's waiting arms. He caught the ball in full stride and took it in for the game's first touchdown.

"That's what I'm talking about!" Conner shouted as he spiked the ball into the ground and then did his version of a victory dance in the end zone. Several of his teammates ran to congratulate him.

"See how the pros do it?" he bragged as he passed Rico to line up for the kickoff.

"Oh yeah? Let's see how you do when I'm guarding you, *hot dog*!" Rico shot back.

"How 'bout you eat my dust like the other guy did!" Conner crowed as he walked away.

Rico's team took the kick and on the next series, drove down to the twenty-yard line. Despite their best efforts, they failed to score due to some good defense and a dropped pass. Following two scoreless drives back and forth by both teams, Rico got the moment he'd been waiting for.

Conner's team had the ball. Again, he pressed the quarterback to throw it his way. "Listen, this time I'm going down the opposite sideline. I'll do a stop and go.

Hit me deep again. I can't wait to show this Rico guy who the captain of our raft is," Conner snickered.

At the line of scrimmage, Rico crouched down low directly across from Conner. The way they glared at each other, even a casual onlooker could see the disdain between them.

"You're going to work up an appetite trying to chase me down, chico," Conner blurted arrogantly. Rico flushed with anger but said nothing. His cold stare revealed what he was thinking.

Conner planned to fake-out Rico with a quick move and then race past him for another catch and score. "Hut-one, hut-two, hut-three, go, go!" the quarterback shouted right before the ball was snapped.

Conner was ready to try his fake-out move, when Rico heard the signal caller shout, "Go, go!" In the blink of an eye, he charged across the line and smashed into Conner so hard that his feet flew out from under him and he was knocked backward and landed square on his backside with a loud thud! Conner tried his hardest to say something, but lacked the air to do so. Rico stood quietly over him as Conner tried to catch his breath and figure out exactly where he was.

Suddenly, the breakfast bell rang out across the camp. Looking down at his vanquished opponent Rico put on his best Hispanic accent and scoffed, "Hey, Señor, chico is looking forward to seeing you later today in the raft. Enjoy your breakfast, amigo."

With that Rico turned confidently and headed off to breakfast. Conner lay groaning on the ground for the next few minutes before some concerned teammates helped him to his feet. With their assistance, he was ushered back to his cabin where he spent the breakfast hour eating his pride and recovering his senses.

Just as Conner was being helped to his cabin, Savi and Jade were headed for the largest building in the center of Camp Arrowhead. It served both as a place where they ate their meals during the day, and where campers hung out or played games in the evening. When they noticed that Conner was injured and being escorted back to his cabin, Jade asked a passerby, "What happened to him?"

"He got clocked on the football field by this guy named Rico," the boy replied.

"What do you mean, he got 'clocked' by Rico?" Savi questioned.

"He got knocked on his butt is what I mean!"

"Who is this Rico?" Jade asked.

"There he is! Right there. He's the one in the black shirt and jeans going into the dining hall."

"Thanks," the girls acknowledged simultaneously as they turned and strolled toward breakfast together. "I didn't see his face, did you, Savi?"

"No," showing her disappointment.

"Well, I guess its time to see who this mystery man is," Jade insisted.

"I agree—I hope Conner's okay though."

"Really… after what he said to you yesterday?" Jade asked in disbelief.

"Don't get me wrong, I don't mean I like what he said to me. I just hope he's okay."

"You're something else, Savi."

"Besides, we may need someone to row the raft later," Savi added jokingly.

Both girls laughed out loud as they opened the door to the dining hall. Walking inside, Jade looked to her left and Savi to her right. They both hoped to get a closer look at Rico.

"Excuse me!" came a voice from behind. When Jade turned around she found herself face to face with Rico for the first time. Neither could speak for a minute; Rico finally broke the awkward silence between them with, "I saw you last night by the fire. I just wanted to say hi...my name's Rico."

Savi saw that Jade was stunned and at a loss for words. So as good friends do, she came to her rescue.

"Hi, Rico. I'm Savi—Jade and I are in the same raft with you."

"Hey, Savi. It's good to meet you. I haven't gone on this level of white water rafting before. It sounds crazy!"

"Yeah, I know! I'm really looking forward to it."

"Me too."

"Well, I guess I'll see you guys later," Rico said looking intently in Jade's direction. Then he turned and walked away.

Before he had taken too many steps, a gentle voice behind him said, "Hey Rico, thanks for saying hi." He spun around at the sound of her voice, and once again seemed struck by her beauty. "I guess I'll see you later," Jade added with a cute smile.

All at once, the camp director burst into the dining hall and shouted, "Is Rico Cruz in here?"

Rico stepped forward and identified himself. "That's me, Mr. Anderson. What's up?"

"I hear you were involved in an incident on the football field earlier?" he said with a scowl on his face.

"It depends on what you call an incident," Rico replied.

"Come this way, young man, you've got some explaining to do." With those parting words, Director Anderson escorted Rico to the office.

Concerned about the confrontation they'd just witnessed, the two girls worried about what might be going on in the office. It wouldn't be long before they found out.

CHAPTER FOUR

Inside the Camp Director's office, Rico sat quietly on a metal folding chair across from Mr. Anderson's desk. The director said he had heard about the incident on the field from the camp nurse. She'd been asked to visit Conner by a few concerned teammates.

After interviewing participants from the game, he was now ready to talk with Rico. "Well, young man, after checking with a few people who saw the whole thing, I now have a better understanding of what motivated your aggressive behavior on the field. The boys I spoke with claim that it was actually Conner Swift who initiated the conflict by insulting you with a racial slur. Is that correct?" He leaned forward.

"Yeah, but it's nothing I haven't heard before," Rico responded with casual indifference.

"Well that kind of behavior is not tolerated here. And neither is the kind of overly aggressive physical response you displayed on the field earlier today."

Rico was smart enough to know that he was better off agreeing with the director than arguing with him. So, he chose to sit quietly and take his medicine while he resisted the temptation to talk back.

After a brief pause Mr. Anderson continued, "I've got a guy down in his cabin who's seeing stars and it's the middle of the day. That's not good, Rico, that's not good at all! A hard hit on the football field is one thing, but knocking a boy silly is way over the top. I need your assurance there will be no more physical altercations between the two of you. Have I made myself clear?"

"Yes sir," Rico replied respectfully.

"And before you go, there's one more thing you need to know. I'll be speaking with Conner later to inform him that if I hear about one more racial comment, he'll be spending the summer in the kitchen on clean up detail."

"Is that it, Mr. Anderson?"

The Director nodded. "That's it."

"Then I'll go and get ready for the rafting trip," Rico declared as he rose to his feet to exit the office.

As soon as he got outside, he noticed Jade and Savi sitting on a nearby bench. It appeared they had been waiting there for a while, their eyes noticeably focused on the office door. When they saw Rico open the door and come out, they jumped up and ran over to him.

"Hey, what happened in there?" Jade asked.

"Not much...Actually, Mr. Anderson is thinking about retirement and was wondering if I'd be interested in applying for the director's job," he informed the girls with a straight face. Upon hearing this, the girls looked first at each other, and again back at Rico. Then all three burst into laughter.

When the laughter died down, Rico decided it was time to pack for the rafting trip that was just a few hours away. Savi and Jade knew they had better do the same, so off they went. As Jade started to walk away she looked over her shoulder in Rico's direction and, just then, he turned to look at her as well. A bit embarrassed, they both shot up a quick wave and then continued on to their cabins, both of them glad to be in the same raft.

Twenty excited campers spent the rest of the morning preparing their backpacks for the white water adventure. Rafters also reviewed the required reading in their rafting safety manual. This was the first group out of five to participate in the white water adventure.

Savi's dad (a former army sergeant) had inserted a "Crisis Only" watertight pouch in her backpack for her to use in the unlikely event of an emergency. Although initially objecting to the extra weight, she now carried the pouch proudly in recognition of her father's thoughtfulness and tenderhearted love.

Savi's mom also contributed to her daughter's backpack in a fun way. She packed a stash of Savi's favorite Fig Newton cookies and some Red Vines, which she carefully tucked into her bulging pack.

Conner was also getting ready for the trip following a morning spent recovering from Rico's bone-jarring hit on the football field. However, his preparations were interrupted by a visit to the director's office. On his way to the meeting, Conner plotted out his strategy to minimize the tongue-lashing he knew he was about to receive.

"Hi, Mr. Anderson," he greeted him with a forced smile when he entered the office. "I heard you wanted to see me."

"Take a seat," the director said as he pointed to the chair in front of his desk, the same one used by Rico earlier. "First, I want to know how you're doing?" he asked with concern. "I heard you took a hard hit on the field this morning."

"I'm doing fine," Conner answered. "I just got the wind knocked out of me, that's all. But thanks for asking."

"That's good to hear. Now let's talk about the issue I brought you here to discuss," the director added ominously. "It's been brought to my attention that you used a racial slur on the football field this morning. Is that true?"

Conner knew this was his moment. He had rehearsed his answer in advance and was prepared for the performance.

"I'm embarrassed to say yes, Mr. Anderson, I did," Conner admitted apologetically. "And I can't tell you how ashamed I am of myself. I've never said anything like that before. It just slipped out." His head dropped for effect. "I was just getting ready to apologize to Rico when he knocked me to the ground so hard I couldn't see straight. I can't remember for sure, but he may have hit me as I was coming up to tell him how sorry I was."

The director looked intently at Conner, probably trying to determine if he was sincere, or just trying to pull a fast one over on him.

"I know what I did was wrong, and I deserve to be punished," Conner said convincingly. "I give you my word, it won't happen again."

Mr. Anderson appeared to take the apology at face value and after explaining to Conner the potential consequences of a future slip up, he moved on to the next subject.

The director informed Conner that he was considering reassigning him to another raft to separate the two boys and avoid another confrontation. Conner didn't want that, thinking to himself, *If I switch rafts, everybody's sure to think that I'm afraid of Rico.* After pleading with Mr. Anderson, and promising the director there would be no more incidents, he was allowed to remain in the raft with Savi, Jade, and Rico.

As he left the office, Conner whispered under his breath, "Award-winning performance. I deserve an Oscar for that one."

CHAPTER FIVE

A pesky mosquito buzzed by Jade's ear as she rifled through her suitcase, annoying her momentarily as she prepared for the impending white water adventure. Living in San Francisco for most of her seventeen years, she was more familiar with the inside of a mall than the inside of a raft. The only boat she'd ever been on was a cruise around the Golden Gate Bridge. Even though Jade did the hard work of getting her white water certification in a simulator class, she still felt she was out of her element.

Jade's family went on vacation often, but they never went to natural settings. They spent their free time exploring cities in the U.S. and around the world. Name a big city and Jade had probably visited there at least once. She'd been to Broadway shows, the world's most famous museums and the finest restaurants both here and abroad. But this was her first venture into the wild. Though a bit anxious, she still looked forward to the rafting trip, along with the other adventures Camp Arrowhead had to offer.

Across the way, Rico did a final check of his gear. Though he'd done very little white water rafting, he was an experienced backpacker and hunter. He had spent several summers camping, hiking, and hunting with his family. That is, before his mother died of breast cancer when he was thirteen. After that, the camping trips halted abruptly. This would be his first time back in the woods since losing his mother four years earlier.

Just then, Mr. Anderson's voice blared over the camp speakers, "Lunch will be served in thirty minutes. All those going on the rafting trip, your safety orientation will begin sharply at one o'clock on the football field. Bring all your gear because you'll be leaving for the river immediately after the orientation. All campers please bring your cell phones, mobile devices, and laptop computers to the storage area to the left of the office before lunch. They will be secured and returned to you on the last day of camp. All such devices are strictly prohibited at Camp Arrowhead, starting at noon today."

Murmurs of protest sprouted up throughout the camp. But they soon died down since everyone realized there was virtually no Internet or cell service available within miles of Camp Arrowhead anyway.

After reluctantly handing in their tech devices and eating lunch, the rafters returned to their cabins to retrieve their gear. They then descended onto the football field for the mandatory safety orientation.

Approaching the field, they saw several rafts sitting on the grass. Each one had a different number painted on it, and standing beside it, an experienced rafting guide designated to lead that team for the duration of the adventure.

Savi and Jade were among the first to arrive at the field and found their raft marked with a red number 9. Both girls were lugging overstuffed backpacks and were relieved to set them down by the raft.

"Hi! I'm Doug Walker," their guide announced. "One of you must be Jade and the other Savi. Now, who's who?"

"Hi, Mr. Walker, I'm Savi," she said in a friendly voice, reaching out to shake his hand.

"Nice to meet you, Savi, but please call me Doug."

"And you must be Jade?"

"I am Mr.—I mean, Doug. Great to meet you."

In the meantime, Conner had discovered that Jade and Savi were friends. Like most of the other boys in the camp, Jade fascinated him and he wanted to befriend her. But he knew that he first had to make amends with Savi. On his way to the field, he plotted his strategy.

Conner spotted the girls near the raft and decided this was his opportunity. "Hey Savi!" he called out a few feet behind her. She immediately turned around and seemed surprised when she saw Conner approaching. As fast as she had turned around, she turned her back on him. "Savi, please, I need to say something."

"Don't do it," Jade broke in.

"Please, I just need a minute," Conner pleaded.

"What is it, Conner? If you can't tell me in front of Jade, I don't want to hear it."

"I just want to apologize for my stupid comments earlier. I think I was trying to impress the guys I was with at your expense. I'm really sorry for what I said."

"It seems like you've been saying a lot of stupid things today," Savi scowled.

"You're one-hundred percent right...I've acted like a loser. I know it's asking a lot, but will you...will you forgive me? I know I don't deserve it, but I'd like a chance to make it up to you."

Savi pondered his words a minute, and in the end she couldn't say no. Her upbringing had taught her the importance of forgiveness, and now she was being challenged to live out what she professed to believe.

"Okay, Conner. I'm going to give you another chance. But don't talk to me like that again. Got it?"

"You've got my word on it," he responded in a convincing tone.

Just then, Rico approached the group. Conner stepped aside while the girls greeted him warmly. Rico and Conner barely acknowledged each other's presence since they were still not on speaking terms.

Now that they had all arrived, Doug introduced himself to the boys and began his safety orientation. "Alright, before we board the bus and head for the launch site, I want you to hear a few vital instructions along with some serious warnings. The Salmon River has another name; it's called the 'River of No Return' because of its swift current. It flows 425 miles through central Idaho and drops more than 7,000 feet before it comes together with the Snake River. In other words, this is serious business," Doug cautioned.

The girls gulped and looked at each other anxiously before Doug continued. "Many people have lost their lives on this river, though I'm happy to say no one from

Camp Arrowhead is on that list. We take pride in our commitment to safety and our spotless record. I've been rafting this river for fifteen years and I've only had a couple of close calls. In both cases, it was because a rafter didn't listen to me. So you need to remember, there's only one leader on this trip and that's me. If you do what I tell you and when I tell you, we'll all be fine. Are we clear?"

"Yes!" each one responded in unison.

"Okay, now each of you has read the safety manual and passed the safety test earlier. So there's no need to repeat the procedure. But I do want to give you a serious word of caution. This river boasts some of the highest class of rapids in the world. Now here's the good news," he paused momentarily. "That's not the part of the river we will be rafting on. Our journey will take us down Class I, II, and III level rapids. You'll find these rapids plenty challenging and adventurous at times, but nothing like the Class IV, V, and VI rapids further down the river," he added in deadly earnest.

Doug looked at them and saw they were visibly nervous. He realized that before his final warning, this might be a good time to relieve some of the tension. So in his own crusty way he went ahead with one of his notoriously bad jokes.

"Knock, knock!"

The group looked at each other in confusion.

Again, Doug repeated, "Knock, knock!"

Finally, Savi took the bait and responded, "Who's there?"

"Fish."

"Fish, who?" Savi asked rolling her eyes.

"Fish you out of the river, if you don't do everything I say," Doug teased with smile.

Teenagers usually wouldn't laugh at a riddle this bad, but their anxiety was at such a peak, they all did. Doug looked proud he had made them chuckle but nonetheless gave them one last piece of instruction and a final warning.

"Tomorrow the bus will pick us up about five miles downstream. That's the only pick up point for forty miles. After that spot, the wilderness has no roads and the river is treacherous with high walls and virtually no way out again for about twenty-five miles. And then you'd be in Vexel's territory. You've all heard about Vexel, haven't you?"

"The last thing I want to think about is Vexel right now," Jade said nervously. "I'm freaking over this river already."

"Okay," Doug replied. "But in all seriousness, if anything happens to me, you must remember, you have to get out of the river before the extraction point marked in red named aptly, 'Last Chance.' For the last quarter mile leading up to the final take out point, warning signs will begin appearing. I know you're all good swimmers but I'm hoping you don't need to prove it," Doug said in a concerned tone.

Jade and Savi looked at one another.

"God forbid, if by some chance you miss the take out spot at 'Last Chance,' you'll be in serious trouble. And I'm not kidding."

He took out his map, unfolded it and began tracing the river's course. "Almost immediately after 'Last Chance,' you'll find yourselves in Class III rapids. About a quarter mile later, you'll come upon a fork in the river. It will come up fast," he cautioned. "Whatever you do, try to stay away from the left side of that fork. The right side is bad, but you've got a chance to get back to shore down river if you can hold on. But if you do go left, you'll hit Class III and IV rapids quickly and eventually a Class V rapid that even experts have a tough time navigating. Those rapids will run you about six miles down the river before you know what's happened."

"Doug, this is a ton of information. Should we be writing it down or something?" Savi asked.

"No, I just want to point out the dangers connected with this river."

He found his place on the map. "After that, you're immediately caught up in Class IV and V rapids for about thirteen miles and that's the worst part. If you're still alive, you'll be twenty-five miles down river and there is a take out point there. Unfortunately, you'll be in heavy wilderness, and a long way from camp. Worst of all, you'll be stranded in Vexel's hunting grounds."

"You're not telling me that you believe Vexel is real, are you?" Jade asked nervously.

"Well, there's something out there. Some kind of vicious man-eating beast has killed three people over the past six years. And that doesn't count all the animal carcasses found, including a huge black bear that something tore apart. I'm not making this stuff up. We call him Vexel, because he has 'vexed' the wilderness to the south of us for the last six years. Even experienced trackers haven't been able to find him. And one of them was his latest victim," the guide lamented. "But if you pay attention to me and do what I say, you shouldn't have to worry about any of that stuff," Doug assured them.

Savi had listened carefully to Doug's instructions. Though she seemed somewhat apprehensive, as were all the others, she had spent plenty of time in the Mississippi woods with her dad and didn't fear water or the wild. Nor was she overly concerned about the guide's warning about the lower river or Vexel because Doug appeared to be a highly competent and experienced guide. Therefore, it seemed unlikely that they would have to deal with any of the potential issues their guide had raised.

After the forty-five minute talk and demonstration, Doug quizzed them on what they had learned. The group passed with flying colors. Next, he assigned each person a "safety buddy." He paired up Rico with Savi, leaving Conner and Jade as partners. The match-ups left Rico disappointed. Quite the opposite appeared to be true of Conner. Not only was he in raft nine, but now he was on cloud nine! Despite his dismay, Rico appeared to be hiding his feelings, not wanting to show Jade his disappointment, or even worse, tip his hand to Conner.

"Well, right on time, here's the bus," Doug noted as he pointed toward the approaching vehicle. "Don't worry about the rafts, they'll be transported to the launch point. Just bring all your gear and put it under the bus," Doug instructed.

"The fun is about to begin. This rafting trip will be the most exciting adventure of your lives!" Doug promised. They were soon to discover just how right their guide's prediction would be.

CHAPTER SIX

The bus trip to the river launch point took about thirty minutes. Savi and Jade sat together toward the front while Rico found his way to a backseat next to a teammate from the morning's football game. Conner chose to be alone a few rows behind the girls, probably not wanting to admit that he was still hurting from the collision with Rico earlier.

After Doug's safety orientation, Savi and Jade were rather quiet. During the bus ride they spent their time trying to recall as much as they could from their previous training. Never more than now did they understand its importance.

"Now I see why we had to go through white water certification before the trip," Jade sighed breaking the silence.

"Yeah, can you imagine getting on this river if you'd never been trained on how to use a paddle? It would be suicide!" Savi responded.

"I hope the training I did pays off," Jade added. "I actually trained inside in a simulator mimicking white water conditions. That's how I learned about paddling, built up my strength, and eventually got my certification."

"You…you mean you've never been on a real river before? You trained inside?"

"Yep, that's exactly what I'm saying, I've never been on a real river," Jade confirmed.

"Well, I hope it was a good simulator!"

Just then the bus turned down a narrow dirt road and for the first time they could see the Salmon River. It seemed peaceful enough at first glance, but they knew looks could be deceiving. Based on what Doug said, this was an especially calm section of the river in front of the launch point. Within a couple minutes the bus reached its destination.

Twenty rafters were on the bus. Each team of four had a highly trained guide in their raft with them. The rafts were scheduled to launch separately at twenty-minute intervals.

The raft, marked with a big red 9 on it, carrying Savi, Jade, Rico, Conner, and their guide Doug, was slated to be the first raft launched at 2:00, just fifteen minutes away. So when the bus arrived, they knew they needed to gather up their gear and immediately head down to the raft for a final safety check. Following the last safe-guard, the long awaited adventure would begin.

Savi and Jade grabbed their gear as quickly as the driver took it out from under the bus. Rico and Conner did the same and soon they were all at the raft. Doug had the teens put on their life jackets, sunglasses, and red safety helmets and then he performed his final safety check.

Rico and Conner hadn't spoken since the football field and nothing changed at the river's edge. Doug got in the raft first and seated himself in the back end. The boys, who each sat on different ends of the middle inflatable seat, followed him. Savi and Jade were last to board and sat side by side on the front inflatable seat. All their gear was strapped in and they each were given a paddle.

"Can you hear my heart beating?" Jade asked Savi.

"Nope…all I hear is my own," Savi admitted. Then she bowed her head and said what most assuredly was a short silent prayer.

"Rico! Conner! You guys ready?" Doug asked.

"I'm good to go," Rico shot back.

"Me too!" Conner added.

"Girls, you good up there?"

"Let's go for it!" Savi yelled.

"Jade?"

"I guess…I'm ready too," she said tentatively.

"Okay, I'm untying us. Right forward!" Doug shouted.

Jade sitting front right bow, and Rico sitting middle right, knew this was their command to paddle and move the raft left. Savi, front left bow, and Conner, middle left, waited for Doug to instruct them.

Everyone knew from their training that if they wanted to turn right, they'd have to paddle on the left side of the raft. If they wanted to move the raft left, the opposite was true. In addition, they were taught vital commands needed to navigate through the rapids and to get safely around obstacles. Other commands they learned included, "all forward" which meant everyone paddles in unison—"all rest," "left back," and "right forward."

"All forward," Doug commanded. Then for the first time everyone's paddle was in the river and the raft surged ahead. "Listen up! Light rapids ahead; Savi and Jade watch for rocks," the guide cautioned.

"We're watching!" the girls yelled back.

Before they saw the upcoming rapids, the thunderous roar of rushing water grew in volume. Turning the raft slightly left, they got their first glimpse of a short stretch of rapids.

"Steady forward," Doug hollered. "Here we go!"

Moments later, their raft soared smoothly through the light rapids. Apprehension mixed with exhilaration showed on their faces.

"Rock left!" Savi shouted.

"Left forward, stop right!" the guide yelled back in response.

Savi and Rico paddled hard while Jade and Conner stopped rowing and withdrew their paddles from the swift waters. The raft veered to the right and shot past a large rock on the left.

"All forward!"

After going around the big rock Savi glanced over at Jade and couldn't help laughing out loud. Jade was so caught up in the intensity of the moment that she didn't realize her sunglasses were cocked over on one side of her drenched face, as gallons of water splashed on her, making it look as if she'd been swimming in her clothes. Savi wished she had her phone so she could capture a picture of her new friend's comical look.

"Rock right!" Jade yelled.

"Right forward, left stop!" Doug commanded instantly.

This time it was Jade and Rico's turn to paddle furiously while Savi and Conner pulled in their paddles. Once again the raft shot safely by a rock jutting out of the river.

"All rest! Good job."

The relieved rafters lifted their paddles from the cool water and breathed a collective sigh of relief. They could see the water was starting to calm. For a brief moment they proudly turned to congratulate each other, knowing they had paddled well. Next they found themselves floating at a steady pace on a relatively light current before hearing the sound of another upcoming rapid.

The same routine played out during the next hour as they navigated a series of four similar-sized rapids. Each one was followed by a short stretch of slower water before it started up again. At the moment, they relished the calm. To everybody's amazement and delight, they performed flawlessly during their initial test on the river. Even so, they were relieved to realize they were approaching their first planned rest stop.

Once on shore, the girls hugged each other in celebration and then sat on the beach for some much-needed rest. Conner plopped down next to them and the trio took turns trading stories about their first encounter on the river. Rico decided to use his break to talk with Doug, hoping to learn from his many years of experience.

The girls acted graciously with Conner, even though he was so inappropriate to Savi and Rico just the day before. Either Savi had truly forgiven him, or she was putting on a good front. Whatever the case, Conner took full advantage of his opportunity. He acted extra nice to Savi and carefully began making his move on Jade.

"I can't believe how great you paddled out there, girls, especially you Jade," Conner said.

"I was watching you when Savi and I weren't paddling. You were really going for it."

"Thanks, Conner, I tried my best," Jade said proudly.

Savi glanced over at Rico and noticed that while he was trying to listen to Doug, he was also keeping an eye on Conner and Jade. It was then she realized how much Rico was beginning to like her friend. For the next few minutes, Conner kept pouring out compliments on Jade, hoping to slowly win her over. By the look on her face, he seemed to be succeeding.

"Okay, gather up everyone."

Once they did, Doug informed them that the next set of rapids were two of the most difficult to navigate on the adventure. He also reminded them of the importance of working as a team, calling out obstacles, and listening to his every command. Everyone nodded, and realized they were about to face the most dangerous waters on this final leg of the first day's journey. Once over these treacherous rapids, it was only a short float to the overnight campsite.

Now that the break had come to an end, they collected themselves and made their way over to the raft.

Following a quick safety check, just as before, Doug led the way as they all climbed back into the raft.

"Everyone ready?"

They all acknowledged that they were good to go. As Doug untied the rope holding the raft, Jade turned to Savi.

"Do you really think the rapids ahead are as bad as Doug told us?"

"I'm not sure, but I think we're about to find out!"

CHAPTER SEVEN

At first, the river was calm and the paddling easy, but everyone's apprehension was already beginning to rise. They knew from experience that everything would change in a matter of minutes.

"Okay, in about a quarter mile we're going to hit the first set of Class II rapids," Doug cautioned. "They come one after another, without much of a break between them," he added. "Then we'll hit the Class III, that's the big one. If we get into any trouble, try to keep the raft balanced and stay low."

"You ready to rock n' roll?" Conner shouted out.

"Just paddle when you're supposed to, *hot dog*!" Rico shot back with a glare.

"Listen to that," Savi said in an ominous tone.

The roar echoed in the distance, except it was much louder this time, even more thunderous. The teens knew they were fast approaching the first set of two Class II rapids that Doug had warned them about.

The intensity of the river changed quickly, as did the raucous rumbling ahead of them. It grew louder with each second.

"Around the next bend I need a strong paddle right. There's a big rock as soon as we enter the first rapid," Doug shouted. "Jade and Rico, you're first!" the guide yelled.

Both teens nodded that they understood, and just then the river turned slightly left. The violent uproar was so overwhelming that Savi and Jade glanced at each other with deep concern but knew there was no way out.

"Here we go!" the guide shouted again. "Now, paddle hard right!"

At his command Jade and Rico started paddling with all their might. Within seconds, the raft was caught up by the first rapid and raced down the turbulent waters.

"Paddle hard right!" the guide yelled again.

In a moment, they flew past a huge rock and shot down the middle of the rapid. The teens were now fully engaged and obeyed every command without question.

"Rock left!" Savi shouted.

"Paddle left!" Doug yelled in reply.

Savi and Conner tried to steer clear of the rock but the backside of the raft hit it. Helplessly they watched and braced for impact.

"Paddles up, hold on!" Doug shouted.

The collision momentarily lifted Savi and Jade off their seats. Both girls screamed as the raft bounced off the rock and turned the raft a bit sideways.

"Paddle hard right! Hard right!" Doug commanded.

Jade and Rico fought hard to straighten out the raft and won the battle. Again, they were in the middle of the river moving swiftly through the torrent. Within a minute, they hit the end of the first set of rapids and now had a moment of desperately needed rest.

"Okay, one down and one to go," Doug said. "Everybody good?"

Still shaken by the collision, the girls could only lift one hand and nod, signifying their readiness.

The roar of the second rapid sounded as frightening as the first. But this time they sailed through it without much difficulty. They avoided every obstacle and paddled brilliantly through the raging rapid. Doug commended them for their efforts and told them they had about a half-mile of calm water to rest before they hit the final Class III rapid between them and the campsite.

"Hey—You guys okay up there?" Rico asked the girls.

"This is so intense," Savi answered with a strong sigh.

"Jade, what about you?" he asked again.

Jade turned toward Rico and immediately burst into tears. Rico quickly leaned forward and grabbed her hand. "You're doing great, Jade! It's almost over. Just one more to go." Rico's soothing presence calmed her.

"Yeah, but it's the worst one," Jade lamented.

"Hey, look at me," Rico said as he slid towards her and took off his sunglasses so she could see his eyes. "I know this is tough. It's tough for me too…You've got this," he assured her. At that moment, if Jade could have hugged Rico she surely would have. But the grip of his hand on hers had to be enough for now.

"Thanks, I'll be okay," Jade replied with a sense of renewed confidence.

Rico released her hand and slid back onto the inflatable bench to his previous position.

Conner had been watching Rico comfort Jade, and seemed mad at himself that he hadn't thought to do it first.

"Conner, you doing alright?" Doug asked.

"Yeah, I'm good," he replied. But he didn't do a very good job of masking his annoyance.

"The last one is about a quarter of a mile ahead. Don't be frightened by the roar. As we get closer, it will sound like a tornado. You have to listen carefully to my commands over the thunder of the river," Doug cautioned.

As soon as Doug finished, from a quarter mile away, everyone heard the clamor of doom. As Doug had predicted the noise was daunting and deafening. The closer they got the louder the roar increased. The howling of a tornado that Doug described couldn't have been more accurate.

"Here we go. Paddle forward. Try to keep us straight." The guide commanded everyone in the raft with short distinct phrases.

The river turned slightly to the right and then they saw the nightmare ahead. The turbulence was like nothing they had seen before. The water appeared completely white and rushed forward at a furious pace, breaking over and against rocks on both sides. The only way through it was a narrow slot between the rocks, which they needed to hit just right, to make it through safely.

"Watch for rocks," Doug warned with a shout. "And hold on!"

As they shot through the tight gap between the rocks, water rose above the raft on both sides. They flew through the first surge and then saw the river bend slightly and reveal a new set of obstacles.

"Paddle left!" Doug yelled over the thunderous roar.

"Hard left!" he shouted again.

"Rock!" Savi screamed.

Water drenched them from every direction. Conner removed his right hand from the paddle for a second to wipe off his glasses.

"Rocks left!" Savi shouted.

Just then the bottom of Conner's paddle smacked against a rock and flew into the air at Doug. The paddle spun and hit him in the face with such force it knocked him unconscious. He fell backwards bleeding on the back of the raft.

"Doug's down!" Rico shouted. "Doug's down!"

"Rocks right!" Jade yelled.

"Paddle right! Hard right!" Rico commanded.

The raft careened out of control down the river. With Savi on the left side, and the only paddler, Conner did his best to hang on to Doug.

"Rock left!" Jade screamed again.

The raft hurled itself into a rock so hard that Conner lost his grip on the guide and Doug flew out of the raft and into the raging river.

"Oh my God! Doug's in the water!" Conner shouted.

The fork in the river that Doug had warned them about earlier suddenly appeared. Both sides looked equally treacherous but they remembered their guide's instructions to stay to the right. Realizing they had two paddlers on the right and only one on the left, Rico yelled over the roar, "Jade, switch sides! You and Savi paddle hard left."

"Where's Doug?" Savi screamed.

"Paddle left or we're going down the left fork," Rico yelled again.

"There's Doug!" Jade cried out.

Doug, now conscious, was being propelled down the river to the right of the raft twenty feet away and slightly behind them. He was face up with his feet pointing down the river, which his experience had taught him was the only way to survive the raging waters.

The raft quickly floated by the final two warning signs before the Last Chance takeout. A few seconds later, to their horror, they zipped past the Last Chance takeout spot.

"Doug!" Savi shrieked.

As hard as they tried, they could not maneuver the raft to the right side of the river's fork. Seconds later, the raft shot through the left side of the fork while Doug floated away to the right.

"Doug! Doug!"

Jade and Savi frantically screamed his name, but it did little good. He was gone. The group realized at that moment that they were on their own, and heading down the most dangerous side of the fork.

"Conner, look for Doug's paddle!" Rico shouted.

"No way! I'm staying down!" he shouted back.

"Rocks left…We're going to hit them!" Savi warned.

"Get low and hold on!" Rico yelled.

CHAPTER EIGHT

The raft smashed against the rocks and would have flipped over except that they all squatted low in the vessel and clung to their safety straps. Within seconds they hit another large rock and again came perilously close to capsizing, but they shifted their body weight just in time to balance out the raft.

The small vessel was now at the mercy of the turbulent waters as everyone hung on for their lives. The group rode the raft like a bucking bronco continuously shifting their weight for what seemed like forever. Finally, the waters slowed a bit in a section of the river surrounded by steep walls. Sadly, the shaken and desperate foursome realized there was no place to land because the sheer rock walls encased the river.

"What are we going to do now?" Jade cried out.

"Try to find your paddle," Savi answered.

Rico scanned the shoreline. "We've got to get off this river," he concluded, "but there's nowhere to land."

"My paddle, it's gone!" Jade screamed.

"Savi, get back here with me," Rico ordered. "Conner, look for Doug's paddle or I'll kick your butt…if we make it out of this alive."

"Just try it!" Conner shouted back. "I've already looked for Doug's paddle and it's gone. And who made you the boss anyway! You don't know anymore than the rest of us. I don't have to listen to you! Who do you think you are?"

"I'm your new babysitter—Now, sit down and shut up!"

Once again they heard the familiar roar of rapids ahead. Savi and Rico now sat opposite one another in the middle seat clinging to the only paddles left aboard. Savi sat on the left side of the inflatable bench and Rico on the right.

"Jade, keep an eye out for rocks. Savi, give your paddle to Conner. And Conner, get up here and help me."

"No way I'm giving my paddle up to Conner," Savi fired back. "He crumbles under pressure."

"Okay then, Savi, it's you and me."

The thunderous rapids ahead grew louder by the second. By now, they had traveled over twelve miles down the river with no foreseeable way out.

"Here we go; just try to keep the nose of the raft down river, Savi."

"Got it."

"You're a brave girl for such a little thing," he said with admiration in his eyes. "Are you ready?"

"Lord, help me!" Savi shouted. "Here we go!"

"Rocks right!" Jade yelled.

Though the next series of rapids was strong, with plenty of big rocks that threatened along the way, they were not as bad as the Class III rapid that ejected

Doug from the raft and caused them to lose two of the paddles.

Savi and Rico did a masterful job of navigating the raft over the next several miles of intermittent rapids. And Jade courageously held on up front and pointed out rocks they needed to avoid.

Then they heard it, a horrific noise like no other they had heard before. Even the Class III rapids had not sounded like this. If the Class III roared like a tornado, this one sounded like three tornadoes. They knew it had to be at least a Class IV rapid, if not worse.

Doug had warned them that in the unlikely event that they missed the Last Chance take out point, they must avoid the left fork of the river no matter what. Unfortunately, they were not able to do so. Frightened and overwhelmed, they now moved swiftly down that perilous side of the river.

The roar was already deafening even from a distance. Savi and Rico knew they had to muster all their remaining strength if they were all going to survive this next series of rapids.

"Savi, we've got to keep the nose in the middle the best we can. That's our best chance. If we hit rocks, pull your paddle up so we don't lose another one."

"Okay."

"Jade, are you ready?"

"I guess so," she said after glancing back at Rico with a look of fear and apprehension.

The first rapid they hit propelled them at a speed that went beyond anything they had experienced before.

They shot down the river like a roller coaster except this ride didn't have tracks or seatbelts. Miraculously, they kept the nose of the raft downstream most of the time and thus averted disaster.

Following the first set of rapids, Savi and Rico were able to take a short break. Suddenly, the river turned right and there on the left they sighted a landing spot about ten feet long. To their dismay, they saw it too late and the river carried them right past it within seconds.

Rico appeared frustrated by Conner's lack of effort.

In a mocking tone he said to him, "How's the ride back there, *hot dog*? Can I get you anything? Maybe some lunch, you must be hungry from all that paddling."

"Shut up, Rico! I don't have a paddle. What do you want me to do?"

"You really want me to tell you?" Rico barked back.

"That's enough you guys! We don't have time for this," Savi scolded them both. "Put on your big boy pants and let's figure out how to get out of this alive," she added in a tone that left no room for misinterpretation.

They figured the raft had gone about twenty miles down river from where they pushed off, and the terrain had changed significantly. Now they were surrounded by a rugged wilderness. It was so thick it looked like night beneath the canopy of trees and dense foliage. The water was still fast but Savi and Rico were quickly learning to paddle and steer their way down the treacherous river. But the hard work had taken a toll on them and they were both exhausted.

"Savi, we've got to figure out how to get off this river. I don't think we can paddle much longer."

"I agree. My arms are burning, like they're about ready to fall off."

"Let's try to paddle to the right side of the river and see if we can toss the anchor into the trees and maybe stop the raft. I mean, what can we lose?"

Savi quickly thought about Rico's idea. "Okay, let's try it," she agreed.

The two weary rafters paddled as hard as they could and moved the raft to the right edge of the river. The tree line came right up to the water's edge, with virtually no riverbank to speak of. Yet, despite their efforts, the raft still moved fast along the water's edge. The current was beginning to strengthen again. If they didn't quickly toss the anchor and catch it in the trees, they might not get a second chance.

"Savi, you paddle hard left and I'll try to toss the anchor to shore."

"Hey, *useless!*" Rico barked at Conner. "Here's my paddle. Get up front left and help Savi paddle and keep us right."

"Pass it to me and I'll help her," he replied.

On Rico's command, Savi paddled with all her remaining strength with Conner helping also. Just then, the current grew stronger and the roar of new rapids ahead told Rico it was now or never. He couldn't wait any longer. He tossed the anchor with all of his might.

"Big rock on the right!" Jade cried out.

The anchor landed between two trees just as the raft was about to pass the huge rock. When it caught, the raft instantly swung hard to the right. It struck the rock so hard that they were flung into the air. But poor

Jade, because she was in front, got the worst. The collision knocked her from the raft into the water and her shoulder hit the big rock. Wincing in pain she found herself wedged between the raft and the rock holding on to the lifeline, which was the rope threaded around the top of the raft.

"Jade's in the water! She's pinned!" Savi screamed.

"Use your paddle and push the raft away from her so she can breathe!" Rico yelled. "I'll try and free her."

"Hold on, Jade, I'm coming!" he shouted.

"I can't hold on!"

"Jade, give me your hand."

"I'm afraid to let go!"

"Jade, give me your hand right now!" Rico commanded her.

Jade felt the strong current dragging her under even with her life jacket on securely. Her strength all but gone, she knew she had no choice. She let go with her left hand and reached for Rico's outstretched hand. His vice grip clenched her wrist and he wasn't letting go. After much difficulty, he managed to get her back into the raft. She was hurt, soaking wet, and traumatized. Her shoulder bled badly, and her back ached from the constant beating she took while pinned against the huge rock.

"Untie your backpacks. Get me the safety kit and bring Jade's pack with you ashore. We've got to get off this raft," Rico said in desperation.

"How?"

"Right over there. See that little ledge on the side of the rock. Once we get there, we can get to shore."

"What about Jade?" Savi whispered to Rico. "She can't do that."

"You let me worry about Jade. You and Conner get your packs and don't forget Jade's. Then one at a time, come to me. Keep the raft balanced in the meantime because I don't want to move her till I have to."

Rico helped tie a rope around Savi's waist and led her to the right side of the raft. He held the rope as she leaped for the small rock ledge.

"Great job, Savi. Now move to that big flat rock and catch the backpacks. Conner will throw them to you one at a time."

Savi not only made it to shore safely but was able to catch all four backpacks as well. Rico untied the rope from his waist that was connected to Savi and she reeled it back to shore and quickly rolled it into a coil for use later. Conner went next. He jumped to the rock ledge with no problem. Now, it was Jade's turn.

"I'm really hurting Rico," Jade complained through her tears, as he stroked her head tenderly.

"I can't jump to the ledge…I'm too scared…I don't want to fall into the water again."

Rico convinced her that this was the only option. The side they were exiting was pinned against the rock. Rico knew that if she fell she'd be within reach between the raft and the rock. But he also understood that if she fell she'd probably drown since she had no strength left and the river current was so powerful.

"Savi, I've taken this rope and tied it around my waist. I'm going to throw the rest of it to you. Tie it around a strong tree as tightly as you can for me."

He shifted his attention to Conner. "Help her secure the line."

Savi and Conner did as instructed. Now Rico was ready to help Jade to the ledge.

"Okay, Jade, you need to get up and sit here a minute so I can tie a rope around you." Rico had tied a sharp hunting knife to the outside of his pack. He used it to cut another piece of rope. This one he tied around Jade's waist. He then tied the line around his own, along with the one attached to the anchor on shore.

"Now, Jade, get up carefully and give me your hand. You've got a long step to the ledge but you can make it. I'll be right behind you," Rico assured her.

"I'm afraid I can't do it!" She was shaking now.

"You've got to try. It's our only hope. I've got you. Just lean forward and I'll hold you with the rope until you're ready to go."

She still looked hesitant. "Ready, Jade?" Rico said. "Go ahead and step over."

Jade leaned forward and placed her left foot on the ledge. She was just about to place her right foot down on the rock when suddenly, she heard Savi gasp. Out of the corner of her eye, Savi saw something coming down the river. She realized what was happening and thought to herself, *Oh God no!* Then she screamed, "Look out!" pointing at the log hurtling in their direction. "Rico, it's going to hit the raft!"

CHAPTER NINE

Rico spun around to see the log barreling down the river toward the raft. Simultaneously, Jade glanced over her right shoulder to look upriver, and that's when she slipped. This time she fell feet first into the water between the large rock and the raft. The current immediately pushed her into the V between the rock and the vessel. Again she was pinned. Although she was tethered to Rico by the rope around both their waists, she was in great pain and struggled mightily.

"I can't breathe," Jade gasped in a broken, wounded voice. "The raft…it's crushing me."

Rico had just turned back to see Jade fall when Savi heard, "WHAM!," as the log hit the back of the raft. The jolt caught Rico off guard because he'd been focused on Jade. The sudden impact knocked him backwards and into the water. Fortunately, he snagged the lifeline as he tumbled over the left side of the raft and clung to it with all his might. Both Jade and Rico winced in pain, as the rope grew taut and tightened around both their waists.

"Rico, try to work your way back around the raft!" Savi shouted. "That will relieve the rope pressure on Jade. I'll go help her!"

Rico nodded and yelled back, "I'll work my way back around!" "Conner, hold on to my rope and pull it when I tell you to!" she commanded.

Savi had tied a rope to a nearby tree and knotted it to her waist clip. "Keep it tight," she instructed Conner as she stepped carefully onto the rock ledge. When she reached it, she knelt down beside Jade who was desperately clinging to the lifeline, now perilously with only one hand. Quickly, Savi grabbed the back strap on Jade's life jacket to keep her head above the water line. Jade was then able to put her other hand back on the lifeline. But by this time, she was struggling for every breath, the weight of the raft pressed up against her chest impairing her breathing.

"I can't…hold on much longer," she moaned.

"Jade can't breathe and she's going under!" Savi screamed. "I've got to cut the anchor line and release the raft. It's crushing her."

"Conner, let go of my rope and come here and hold on to Jade. I've got to cut the raft loose."

Conner moved as quickly as he could on the slippery ledge. Savi knew there was no time to spare. So as soon as he was close enough to grab the strap on the back of Jade's life jacket, she snatched her pocket knife from her pack and without warning or hesitation, jumped into the water between the rock and the raft. She tried to snag the lifeline at the back of the raft, but the swift current carried her to the side instead.

She then began the laborious task of working her way against the current to the rear of the vessel.

"Rico, are you alright?" Savi shouted.

"I'm good. I'm almost to the back."

Rico worked his way back around the raft as fast as he could using the lifeline. Every inch he moved lessened the rope pressure on Jade. Eventually he made it to the back of the raft and carefully went around Savi, who was now also at the rear of the vessel. He then made his way to the V where Jade and Conner were trying to hold on.

Right away, Rico saw that Jade was in bad shape. "We've got to get the raft off of her now."

"Rico!" Conner yelled. "When Savi cuts the anchor line and frees her, you try to lift her as far as you can to me. I'll pull her out of the water and onto the ledge."

"Savi, hurry! Cut halfway through the anchor line and then on the count of three finish the cut!" Rico shouted.

"Okay...I've got it cut halfway."

"Ready? One...two...three!"

The final cuts caused the line to pop when it snapped. Instantly, the current swept the empty raft down the river until it was out of sight.

When Savi let go of the lifeline, the force of the water instantly swept her into the big rock with the ledge, but she had prepared herself for that and hit it squarely feet first. She hurriedly reeled in the slack on her rope and knotted it. Dangling in the river at the end of the rope, she realized the only thing between her and death was the rope and a tree. Gradually, she worked her way to the widest part of the ledge. After taking time to catch her breath and regain some strength, she pulled herself out of the water and rolled herself onto the ledge. Exhausted, she watched as Rico and Conner worked together to rescue Jade.

Finally, Jade was lifted out of the water. Conner and Rico hoisted her on the same rock ledge as Savi. She was fully conscious but still in a bad way. Savi crawled close enough to her to touch one of her blood soaked gloves. Jade apparently knew it was Savi but clearly didn't have the strength to turn her head.

Rico was the last one to make it on to the ledge. He had watched Savi mount the rock and inched his way to the wider part of the edge and lifted himself on to it. Once everyone had moved safely to dry ground, the focus shifted to Jade. They bandaged the rope burns on her waistline and treated her wounded hands, back, and shoulder. Though battered and hurt, she was already breathing better and a tint of color had returned to her wet but still beautiful face.

Once they were convinced that Jade would be okay, the remaining trio collapsed inside the tree line and took the next hour or so to revive themselves.

Feeling a bit better, Jade was now able to sit up. "This is so messed up! I don't think I can walk, let alone, hike."

Savi leaned forward and replied, "Don't worry about that now, Jade. We're not going anywhere for a while."

"Here, lay back down. Just rest and we'll figure out what to do," Savi said gently while stroking her head, which she continued to do until Jade fell asleep.

The three distanced themselves far enough away as not to disturb her, but close enough to keep her in full view.

"Can you say, we are so screwed?" Conner grumbled.

"Oh great, just what we need from you, Conner, more bad news." Rico fired back in a frustrated tone. "You're always so negative."

"Okay, let me reword my statement. We are so *positively* screwed. Is that better?" Conner said as he glared at Rico.

"You two need to stop this bickering now," Savi demanded. "If we want to get out of this alive, we need to work together as a team." She eyed Rico and Conner. "You need to quit acting like two-year-olds, and I mean it." She stood with arms folded and glared at both of them. "I don't care how much you don't like each other. You need to shake hands and get over it. You've both said and done enough cruel things to one another. We need to depend on each other, now more than ever. And that includes you two…Got it?"

As much as it was obvious that he hated the thought of shaking Conner's hand, Rico knew that Savi was right. Mustering all the courage he could, he lifted his hand and extended it to Conner.

Conner stood for a moment and looked at Rico's hand and then heard, "Conner."

The two boys shook hands, though, not very convincingly.

"Now that's better."

By 6:30 that night, word had reached Camp Arrowhead that Raft 9 was missing. Rescue crews were immediately dispatched down the river. At the fork just past the Last Chance takeout, the rescue crews chose to search the right side of the river, knowing that the guide would have told them to stay right.

At nightfall, after an afternoon and evening of seeing no one and no raft or wreckage, the rescuers started fearing a bleak outcome. To make matters worse, a violent weather system that had shifted direction was now heading their way. This meant a more extensive search team could not be deployed before morning.

Savi opened the sealed package in her backpack marked "Crisis Only" that her dad had insisted she carry. Grateful for his forethought and wisdom, she now surveyed the package's contents that included a small box of wooden matches, a butane lighter, a compass (that she clipped to a metal ring on her vest), ten energy bars (four of them she put in her vest), a thin plastic tarp, and a miniature flashlight.

Almost miraculously, Jade was up and walking about. She was still very sore and shaken but three hours of sleep had helped her a lot. Conner and Rico were out gathering broken branches for the fire Savi had started. It was now getting colder and their damp clothes added to their discomfort.

Everyone gathered around the warm fire hoping it would help them forget about the dire situation they found themselves in, at least for now, and lessen the bite of their first night in the chilly air. Rico spent his time carving a point on a good size length of wood. It was obvious he was making a spear.

Meanwhile, Savi decided to open up the Fig Newton cookies in her pack since they were all so hungry. When she did, the scent of sugar and shortening filled their nostrils.

Suddenly, they heard a loud rustling of bushes and branches snapping downriver not far from where they had set up their makeshift camp.

"What was that?" Savi whispered anxiously. "It couldn't be Vexel, could it?"

"Quiet." Rico rebuked her with a hush. He raised the tip of his nearly finished spear.

Again, they heard more noise in the woods. This time they knew it was getting closer.

CHAPTER TEN

Rico and Savi's backpacks were near at hand. But Jade and Conner's were propped up against a tree between them and the frightening sounds coming from the woods.

Rico leaned towards the terrified group and spoke in a whisper, "Savi, you and Conner help Jade and take these two backpacks quietly upriver about three-hundred yards; that's about three football fields. Then make a hard left and go straight inland about two-hundred yards. When you get there, wait for me. I'll grab the other two packs and then catch up with you. No matter what happens, just keep going. I'll find you where I told you to go. Leave the fire as it is and go now."

"Rico, forget those two packs," Savi whispered back.

"No, you guys go…now!"

Grabbing Rico's hand she pulled him toward her and cautioned him, "Be careful. Those packs aren't worth your life."

Conner helped Jade to her feet and led the way up the left side of the river with her in tow and in pain. Savi trailed close behind, guarding the rear while keeping an eye out for Rico.

Meanwhile, Rico, with his spear in hand, moved stealthily toward the backpacks leaning against the tree. He could hear by the menacing sounds coming from the woods that whatever was out there was big and getting closer. He snatched the packs off the tree and started moving as quietly as he could in the direction he had sent the others.

Suddenly in the trees behind him, about thirty-yards away, a deep growl followed by a huge belted roar stopped him dead in his tracks. Terrified, he was sure he heard the sound of a bear approaching. He remembered reading about Camp Arrowhead and a hundred known grizzly bears in the area of northeastern Idaho. He hoped and prayed that this wasn't one of them.

Disregarding his own advice about being quiet, he ran past the smoldering fire and through the woods upriver. After he was a good distance from the campsite, he crouched down and looked back at the camp from behind a small group of trees. He was horrified to see a bear, but at least it wasn't a grizzly. Instead, a medium-size black bear was visible in the dying firelight.

The bear slowly made its way through the camp sniffing about, undoubtedly looking for something to eat. Recognizing the danger at hand, Rico slinked away...hoping not to draw the bear's attention. He avoided notice and then decided it was safe to run. His goal now was to catch the others and warn them about the prowling marauder.

After he had gone about three hundred yards, he turned left and started heading inland, away from the river. Then he heard a branch snap no more than ten yards ahead of him. Instantly, he stopped. Crouching down again he looked in the direction of the noise. To his delight, he saw Savi moving through the woods up ahead.

"Savi!" he shouted in a whisper.

She turned, and to her surprise and relief saw Rico approaching. For the first time, without thinking twice, the two hugged.

"Listen. There's a black bear out here. I saw him go through our camp. We've got to get as far away from the water as fast as we can. This must be a passageway where bears come down from the mountains to feed at the river," he speculated.

"Or he sniffed out our food," Savi countered.

"Maybe, the scent of the cookies…Is the package sealed?" Rico asked Savi.

"I think so," she whispered, "let me check."

"Hurry, we've got to get moving," Rico said impatiently.

Savi put down her backpack and opened the flap to check the package. Suddenly, the bear roared again and he wasn't that far away. Savi grabbed her pack just as Rico grabbed her arm and the two of them started running in the direction of the meeting place.

"Rico, we left Conner's pack!"

"Leave it for now. We've got to get out of here," he insisted. "I think the bear is tracking us."

In just a couple of minutes, they caught up with Conner and Jade. As happy as they all were to be reunited, this was no time to celebrate.

"Where's my backpack?" Conner asked in an exasperated tone.

"We had to leave it behind," Rico replied.

"How come you still have yours?"

"Because I was wearing it when we heard the bear," Rico declared.

Rico then told Conner and Jade about the black bear adding to their already high level of anxiety. Knowing the degree of danger all four of them now found themselves in, they scurried off looking for some place to hide from the hungry bear, anyplace. They moved as fast as the night and terrain allowed. Horrified, they heard the bear roar again in the distance.

Rico knew that he possessed the only weapon that could possibly protect them from an animal as large as a bear. He also knew that in order to survive, they needed to stay close together and find adequate shelter.

The moon provided enough light that they could actually see reasonably well. All of a sudden, the trees gave way to a circular clearing about a hundred feet around. On the other side was a large cluster of rocks. They were all weary from running and Jade was now in serious pain and could run no more. Scared stiff and tired, the group decided to head for the rocks and hide. Suddenly, they heard another roar, this time definitely closer.

Conner noticed an indentation that looked like a cave within the huge rock formation. When they got close to it, they saw that it was indeed a cave and soon discovered that it was about four-feet wide and ten-feet deep and covered by a large boulder that served as a roof. For better or worse, there was only one way in or out.

"Give me the backpacks," Rico demanded. Hurry! We've got to get the food away from us."

"Let's just take the food out," Conner suggested.

"We don't have time for that," Rico warned. "Give the packs to me now!" he ordered again.

Rico traded his spear for the backpacks. Then he took off running to the right side of the clearing. He left the packs at the edge of the clearing, so they were still visible from the cave. Then he hurried back to the rock shelter.

Savi did her best to comfort Jade, while Rico and Conner kept watch at the entrance. It was quiet for about five minutes, and then the loudest roar they had heard yet broke the silence. Suddenly, a medium-size black bear emerged from across the clearing. Conner had to hold back a gasp when he saw the scary animal. The bear stopped and stood fully erect on its hind legs. Peering from the cave, they could see it was at least seven feet tall. Both boys' hearts raced wildly. They were glad that the girls were deeper in the cave and could not see the hungry beast.

All at once, the bear bent back down and began walking and sniffing his way around the clearing. Eventually he worked his way over to Savi's backpack and began to rip at it with his mighty claws. In seconds, the contents of the bag were scattered everywhere as the hungry bear searched for food. Savi's cookies were his first find. He ripped the package open with his claws and lowered his head to munch on the tasty morsels. Then he found and partly demolished the "Crisis Only" pack with a few energy bars still tucked inside of it.

"Well, there goes *your* backpack, Savi," Conner whispered. "Two down, two to go," he added with a smirk.

Rico turned and looked at him with a stare that Conner had seen only once before, back on the football field. He quickly looked away from Rico and decided it was best to drop the subject.

After the bear was satisfied that he had stripped Savi's pack of food, he looked up and surveyed the clearing again. He then started smelling and tearing at the remaining two bags. At the same moment, Savi tried to help Jade sit up to take a drink. As she did, Jade let out a gasp from the pain of moving. The bear heard the sound and quickly turned his head in the direction of the cave. He stared for a moment and then stood up again, sniffing the air. After a few seconds he began walking, with purpose, toward the cave.

Rico slowly raised his spear and pointed it forward.

"Conner, get behind me," he whispered in desperation. "Here's my knife. If anything happens to me, you've got to protect the girls."

The bear moved across the clearing and then picked up a scent that told him that he was not alone. He started sniffing his way around the rocks until he was just a few feet from the cave. He was determined to find the intruders his nose had detected.

Near the opening of the cave, the dark creature moved to the left and stood up again. He sniffed around a little more until his nose told him to look in a different direction. When he did, his eyes fixed on Rico, the lone guard at the mouth of the cave. The bear snarled and roared. He opened his jaws wide and lunged at Rico!

CHAPTER ELEVEN

Anticipating the bear was about to charge him, Rico held firmly onto his spear, took a step back into the cave, and assumed a defensive position. He gripped the spear tightly with both hands and raised the tip upward towards his adversary. The snarling beast swung at him with outstretched claws. The bear let out a growl when he missed his target the first time and swung again furiously. This time, the beast hit the outstretched spear and nearly knocked it out of Rico's hands. Rico yelled as loud as he could and jabbed at the bear several times with the tip of the spear. For a moment, his tactics worked and the animal backed away, letting out a vicious snarl.

Rico understood that if the bear got into the cave, everyone was dead. At the same time, he also realized he couldn't fight him off for long. So with a surge of courage, he pulled his spear all the way back hoping to lure the bear towards him. Sure enough the beast moved closer. Just as he lunged at him, Rico surprised the attacker by thrusting his spear forward, plunging it into the side of his stomach. The wounded animal's piercing groans chilled him to the bone. The bear backed away momentarily, then, as if it had come to a realization that it was bigger and stronger, the wounded beast became even more aggressive.

"Conner, if he gets in here you'll have to keep stabbing him!" Rico shouted. "Don't stop till he's dead."

During the battle, the petrified girls were curled up together in the backmost part of the cave. If they could have squeezed closer together inside, they would have. They clearly heard the horrible commotion at the entrance, but they couldn't see the bear from their position, nor did they want to. Conner stood directly behind Rico as his terrified backup. He was the last line of defense if the bear got through Rico.

Even in the moonlight, it became apparent the predator was bleeding heavily. Rico was determined to severely wound or kill the bear, so that they might have a chance to escape. Again he reached back as far as he could with his spear, tempting the bear to rush at him. He didn't have to wait long. The snarling bear stepped closer for his final attack. When he got close enough, Rico lunged at him and drove the spear deep into the center of the bear's gut. The creature's response was immediate and instinctual. It swiped at Rico with its claws, cutting into his left arm and knocking him to the ground inside the cave.

Seeing that Rico had been knocked down, Conner leaped forward with hunting knife in hand and stabbed the bear three times in the leg. As he was doing so, the bear clawed him on the left side of his face and he too crumpled to the ground screaming. Now both boys were wounded and bloodied on the floor of the cave.

With Rico and Conner injured, Savi knew she had to act without hesitation. Terrified, she pulled out her knife with trembling hands and began making her way toward the cave's entrance expecting to encounter the bear. When she got to the opening, she was relieved to see the creature hobbling away from the cave toward the edge of the clearing. He moaned loudly with every painful step.

Rico's spear was still lodged in the bear's stomach and the three knife wounds that Conner inflicted had damaged his left leg severely. The bear pawed continuously at the spear in its midsection leaving a trail of blood behind. Finally after several attempts, he dislodged it and the bloody spear fell to the ground. Howling and growling, the wounded animal continued across the clearing until he finally disappeared into the woods.

Savi knew she had to find one of the medical kits quickly, so she could tend to the wounded boys. She crawled out of the cave entrance, surveyed her surroundings, and then darted across the clearing toward the mangled backpacks. The bear had done its work. Savi's backpack was damaged beyond repair and its contents scattered everywhere. Rico and Jade's packs were mauled but still usable. After sifting about the debris, she finally found the two medical kits, put them in the two remaining backpacks, and headed back in the direction of the cave. On her way, she found Rico's bloody spear lying on the ground. She picked it up and brought it back with her.

Conner's face was bleeding profusely. With a deep gash three inches long on the left side of his face, Savi was glad he couldn't see himself in a mirror. Otherwise, he would know that his face would be scarred for the rest of his life. Her hands shook as she dabbed the disinfectant over the nasty wound. He winced in pain but knew the treatment was necessary to prevent infection. Once she finished, Savi put her arms around Conner and whispered in his ear, "You were brave tonight. Thanks for protecting us."

Rico had also suffered a terrible injury, but it wasn't as bad as it first appeared. Despite the pain that wracked his body, after his wound was cleaned and dressed, he discovered he had full use of his left arm.

"Hey Conner, you did good," Rico said in a complimentary tone as they touched knuckles together.

"You too, man," Conner countered. His expression changed. "Do you think that was Vexel?"

"I'm not sure," Rico admitted. "But if Vexel is any fiercer than that bear, I sure don't want to meet *him*."

"What should we do now?" Conner asked, following Rico back into the cave while pressing his hand against the blood-soaked bandage on his face.

"I think we should stay here for the night," he said to the others. "We're all hurting and too exhausted to travel."

"What if the bear comes back?" Conner asked.

"Grab the spear and follow me. We'll go over there and salvage what we can from the mess of backpacks in case he does."

The two left the cave and headed for where the bear had done his work. They could see from across the clearing that their belongings were strewn everywhere.

After leaving the cave, they kept looking back, ensuring no unwelcome animals threatened the girls. Quietly and deliberately, they picked up what they could and made their way back to the safety of their hiding place.

Once they got settled in, Conner and Rico agreed to take two-hour shifts guarding the entrance. They chose to exclude Savi from the rotation knowing that she and Jade were already fast asleep and totally spent. Conner took the first shift hoping for an uneventful couple of hours.

The first two hours passed by surprisingly fast. Other than the chirping of crickets and the occasional hooting of owls, all was quiet. Conner looked down at his watch and decided it was time to wake up Rico for his shift. He gently roused him and then lay down in the cave himself to get some much-deserved rest.

Suddenly, in the distance way upriver, brutal sounds of animals fighting shattered the fragile calm that had settled over the cave. The horrific noise startled everyone awake. The fierce battle waged for a couple of minutes before an awful sounding yelp-like howl pierced the night air, followed by a deafening silence.

Jade sat up, terrified. "What was that?"

"I'm not sure," Rico replied, "but it was pretty far away. I don't think we have anything to worry about for now."

"Go ahead and get some sleep. I'll keep watch. The morning will be here before we know it!"

Savi got up and stepped over Rico holding the knife firmly in her hand.

"What are you doing?" he whispered in an annoyed tone.

Savi stopped and turned back. "I've got to get some things."

She quietly darted across the clearing until she came upon her shredded backpack. Bending down and sifting through the debris field, she picked up a few items and put them in her vest pocket and then quickly returned to the cave.

"What was that?" Rico scolded upon her return.

"I told you, I needed to get some things."

"What things?"

"If you must know," Savi responded. "I picked up some pouches of dried food my dad packed me, a small plastic tarp, my mini flashlight, some stuff from my medical kit, and…my pocket Bible."

Rico's eyes widened. "Bible…what are you going to do with that?"

"Hello," Savi shot back. "I read it! Duh!"

Savi went back into the cave and sat down next to Jade who was still reeling from her near death experience in the river. Curled up in the cold corner alone, she had finally fallen asleep again after the night's trauma. Savi sat down quietly next to her and bowed her head for a moment. Then she lay down on the chilly ground, and within minutes was also fast asleep.

CHAPTER TWELVE

A warm golden sunrise broke through the trees and ushered in a new morning. A flock of Canadian geese honked loudly as they flew overhead in their characteristic V formation. The squawking of the geese woke Jade. She looked around and immediately let out a loud gasp when she saw the blood-soaked bandage on the side of Conner's face. The sound startled Savi, and she, too, woke up.

Savi reached for one of the remaining medical kits to get fresh gauze so she could redress Conner's wound when he awoke. He was beginning to stir, so she waited for a moment until he was fully awake. She knelt down next to him and, once she took off the bandage, examined the injury.

"The wound is really swollen." Savi took out a cotton ball and poured some peroxide on it. "This will help disinfect it…but it might sting."

Conner flinched a couple of times. "Ow…that hurts like crazy."

"I know, but it's got to be done. We can't take the chance of an infection setting in. Now suck it up and hold on."

He did as he was told. In no time, Savi had put on a new bandage. She then did the same for Rico's arm as he guarded the entrance to the cave.

Savi looked out at the sun's rays shining between the trees. A light mist hung low in the air. In the glow of morning, the woods looked harmless and innocent, but she knew that appearances were sometimes deceiving.

Once everyone was fully awake, their first priority was finding food and water. They were all hungry since they hadn't eaten anything but cookies since lunchtime the day before.

The night before, Savi had salvaged three small bags of dried food her dad had placed in her pack. When mixed with hot water the ingredients expanded and became a meal. They were the same kind of dry rations he had used in the military. She recalled that he'd given her chicken and noodles, spaghetti and beef stroganoff. Because the pouches were sealed, the bear had ignored them.

Rico and Savi left the cave and returned once again to the area where the bear had mangled the backpacks. After searching a few minutes, to their relief, they found another food pack unopened. Now assisted by daylight, they collected everything of value and returned to the cave. In the process of searching, they found two intact water bottles and the lighter from Savi's tattered "Crisis Only" pack.

Rico feared the smell of food might attract predators, so he led the group up river a few hundred yards. After gathering some sticks, he used the lighter to start a small fire. Then they poured some water into a tin canteen cup and heated it over the flame. Once hot, they poured it into the pouch and waited for the contents to soften. Each person took turns sharing bites with the two forks and one spoon Rico had recovered. Though it wasn't much in terms of portion size, all of them were grateful to get a little something to eat and drink that morning.

While making their way back to the cave they came upon a gruesome site.

"Oh my gosh!" Jade gasped as she looked down at the huge brown mutilated carcass.

"That's so disgusting," Savi said, holding her mouth. "I'm going to puke," she warned...and then she did.

Savi vomited up her breakfast and then did her best to clean herself up.

"Is that the bear from last night?" Conner asked as he surveyed the dead creature.

Rico took a close look at the mutilated carcass and answered, "Yeah, that's the same bear. See...there are the knife marks on his left leg."

"What in the world could have done this to him?" Conner questioned, with a look of astonishment on his face.

Everyone knew the answer to Conner's question, but no one wanted to be the first to say it. Finally, he answered his own question with another question. "Could it be Vexel?"

The sound of the name, Vexel, sent chills running down his spine and judging by the looks on everyone else's faces, it did the same to them. Rather than wait around for an answer, they high-tailed it back to the cave and tried to figure out what they should do next.

Just then, from up the river, no more than a few hundred yards away, they heard the distinct thumping of a helicopter. They guessed that it was looking for them, but they were too far away from the river to be seen. They also didn't know that their abandoned raft had been found that morning, nearly eighteen miles downriver from their current position. Because of the violent rapids and empty raft, the rescuers began to fear the worst and assumed the rafters had probably drowned. Rather than give up the small sliver of hope that still remained, the rescue team sent three helicopters out in different directions. Despite their airborne vantage point, the dense forest and rugged terrain made it difficult to see much of anything.

Nonetheless, Rico sprung to his feet. "If I hurry, they might see me," he said as he turned and ran for the river. "Over here!" he shouted and waved.

Unexpectedly, the copter banked left and headed in the other direction. Savi, Conner, and Jade finally arrived at the river behind Rico just as the helicopter faded from view. The four stood there speechless and devastated. Less than a minute later, the sound of the copter was gone.

The group now had a difficult decision. Should they risk staying put and running into more predators, and maybe even Vexel, while waiting to be rescued? Or should they undertake the long and tedious journey through the wilderness and trek back to Camp

Arrowhead? After a lengthy discussion, they came up with a plan.

The group decided that Rico and Conner would return to the river and the scene of the raft accident. At the water's edge, they would tie Savi's shredded backpack to a tree hoping it might be spotted by a rescue raft moving down the river. Though they considered their plan inventive, what they didn't know was that a rescue crew had just floated past that site. When they didn't see any traces of the missing teens, they continued down river to search elsewhere.

Upon Rico and Conner's return to the cave, the group continued to huddle together and talk about their options. They came to the conclusion that it would be best if they stayed a couple of days to recover from their injuries before they began the long journey back to camp. Sitting in the cave together, they collectively pondered their precarious situation.

"Do you think we're going to die out here?" Jade asked without hesitation.

"No way!" Savi shot back. "We're going to get through this together."

"Savi's right," Rico chimed in. "We'll probably get rescued. But if we don't, we'll figure this out on our own. Besides, we all came for an adventure, right?"

"So why did you come here, Rico?" Conner asked while holding the side of his face.

"I don't know. I guess the woods and camping bring back good family memories. I mean…when my mom was still alive."

"What happened to her?" Jade asked.

"She died of cancer…then everything changed. My dad didn't come home as much after that, and I ended up taking care of my two younger brothers and little sister. I guess my dad thought I needed a break and that some time away in the mountains would take my mind off everything."

The others looked at Rico sympathetically. They could tell he didn't often let others this deep inside. After a moment, Jade, who sat next to him, reached over and placed her hand softly around his shoulder and squeezed it gently. Rico bowed and shook his head back and forth as if scolding himself for being so vulnerable.

He lifted his head and turned toward Jade. "What about you? Why did you come to Arrowhead?"

"I feel kind of embarrassed answering that question after hearing your story…My reason feels so selfish," she said with a sigh.

"Don't worry about it, Jade, you can tell us," Savi insisted.

"Well, I'm a girl in a Chinese family that values boys and men. When I was old enough to understand that, I discovered that I was a 'mistake.' My parents wanted another boy, but they got me. Ever since I can remember, I've been a disappointment to both my parents but especially my mother. She constantly reminds me where I fall short. In her mind I've always been and will always be a failure…Part of me started wondering if it's even worth living. Then a friend told my parents that I started cutting myself. They freaked out and decided to find somewhere to send me so as not to shame the family. They got me certified as quickly as they could and shipped me off to Arrowhead. I hope here maybe I can at least prove something to myself," she concluded with tears streaming down her cheeks. Jade covered her face with her hands and lowered her head.

The others quickly scooted over to her, and with a keen sensitivity not to touch her wounded shoulder, consoled her for the next few minutes.

"We all think you're special, Jade. I don't care what anybody else says," Savi assured her.

"You're one of the nicest girls I've ever met" Conner added.

"I don't think you're that nice, but you sure are pretty," Rico joked.

Everyone giggled, including Jade.

After a while, Jade looked over at Conner and urged him to share, "Two down and two to go. What about you, Conner? What's your story?"

He hesitated at first and then began, "My story is simple. Every summer my parents travel somewhere in Europe. They find new places to dump me off every year. This year I beat them to the punch and told them I wanted to come to Camp Arrowhead."

"Why Arrowhead?" Rico asked.

"All my life, everything I've ever wanted…has been handed to me. I've never really worked for anything…" his voice trailed off.

"Go on," Savi urged him. "There's nothing to be embarrassed about."

Conner leaned forward. "It's hard to say."

Jade motioned with her hand. "Come on, try."

"Okay, I'll try…The fact is I'm tired of having everything but feeling like it doesn't belong to me. I envy people like the ones who work for my father. They work hard and earn their money. Nobody gives them anything. I'm sick of being told I was born with a 'silver spoon' in my mouth, even though it's true. I guess I just wanted to do something on my own to prove I can."

Rico gave Conner a light smack on the arm. "Hey, you proved you could do something last night. If you hadn't stabbed that bear after I got knocked down, I don't know what would have happened."

"Yeah and now look at my face. I don't need to look in a mirror…I can already tell it's scarred for life. That will really turn all the girls' heads, huh?"

"Conner, you'll always be handsome even with a scar," Jade said in a reassuring tone.

"This is so messed up," he replied exasperated.

"It is what it is, Conner. You can't change it now. Anyway it's probably not as bad as you think. Don't you know that girls think scars are hot? Have you seen mine?"

Rico then lifted up the bandage on his left arm and winced in pain while doing so. He showed them the wound the bear had inflicted on him the night before. Doing his best to mask his discomfort, he playfully taunted the girls, "Come on, look at this soon to be scar, its pretty sexy, right?"

The girls squirmed at first when they saw Rico's wound, then giggled at his good-natured ribbing. Conner laughed as well and seemed to recover a bit from his distress over his facial wound.

Suddenly, from outside they heard the distinct sound of the helicopter coming quickly down the river again. This time, Rico didn't hesitate. He sprinted from the cave and ran for the river. He headed straight toward the sound of the copter as fast as his feet would carry him. But when he broke through the tree line and got to the river, again it was too late. He heard the distant rotors of the rescue chopper fade like they had before. He made his way back to the cave with the stark realization that the time for them to be rescued was running out!

CHAPTER THIRTEEN

Despite their disappointment, the group agreed to use the cave as a refuge and place to recover for the next couple of days. They concluded that staying close to the accident site might increase their chances of being spotted.

Gathering a bunch of downed branches with the leaves still on, they covered the cold hard dirt floor in the cave. And just in case they were attacked again, they did their best to fortify the entrance. They placed several long branches with the tips sharpened and pointed them outward from the cave entrance. In addition, Conner followed Rico's lead and found a long straight solid tree branch and using his pocketknife, carved it into a spear.

Even though Rico's shoulder still really hurt, he knew he needed to suck it up and think about helping the group survive. Earlier, he had managed to salvage his collapsible fishing rod along with his reel and a small tackle box from his mauled backpack. And now, it was time to put them to good use.

"I'm going to see if I can catch us some dinner," he said to no one in particular.

Concerned, Savi objected, "Don't go alone. Let me come with you. I don't think any of us should be off too far away by ourselves. Besides... I can help."

Rico looked at Savi's cute but worried little face and smiled. "On one condition. Here's the deal. I'll catch 'em, and you clean 'em."

"What? That's the dirty job," she protested. "How 'bout I catch 'em, and you clean 'em?"

"You said you would help. Do you want to go or not?"

"Okay, flame down *sparky*...It's a deal," she fired back. "But you better catch some."

Leaving Conner and Jade behind in the cave, the two slipped quietly away and made their way to the water's edge. They climbed over some rocks that jutted over the river and ended up sitting on a big flat one about three feet above the swift current. While Rico prepared his rod and reel, Savi opened the small tackle box and looked over the lures inside. A green one with black dots and a silver stripe caught her eye and she took it out.

"Here, use this one. It will catch us a trout."

"How do you know so much about fishing?" Rico asked.

"Me and my dad fish all the time back in Mississippi."

"But how do you know there are trout in this river?" he quizzed her.

"Because we looked online to see what kind of fish were in this river. We discovered the water is too cold for bass and most other fish but perfect for trout because they like cold water."

"Wow, aren't we so smart?!"

Savi took the playful ribbing and went on. "And the reason I gave you that lure is because it's made to catch large trout."

"Really? Okay, let's try it and we'll see."

Rico tied the lure Savi had given him to the end of his line and began casting it out and then slowly reeling it back in. The lure was weighted, so it sunk down a few feet into the water. Not more than a few minutes later the small rod jerked forward.

"I think I've got one!" Rico yelled. "It feels pretty big...I told you we should use this lure," he said with a big grin. "You ready to clean, girl?"

"You reel it in and I'll make it pretty," Savi promised.

After a short fight, Rico landed a beautiful three-pound rainbow trout. He watched in amazement as Savi used her knife to cut off the fish's head and then slit its belly open to clean out the guts, which she promptly threw in the river.

"You're one of the best fishing buddies I've ever had," he said as he scratched his head in astonishment.

"Glad to hear it. Next time I'll catch 'em and you clean 'em."

"You got a deal," he said with an exaggerated nod of his head.

Feeling encouraged by his success, Rico threw his line back in the river a second time. And just like before, another trout lunged at the lure and took the hook. He reeled the fish in close to Savi who snagged the slippery critter, and per her agreement, cleaned it. After she cleaned the second one, she washed her hands in the cool river to get rid of the awful fishy smell.

The two of them decided to cook up the fish there at the river's edge to keep the aroma as far away as possible from the cave. Gathering some sticks and pine needles, they piled them up, and using Savi's lighter, made a small fire. Rico carved a sharp tip on a branch and skewered the fish onto it. He then roasted them over the flames. Once the fish were cooked, they doused the fire with water to ensure it was out.

Rico and Savi then headed back to the cave with their prized provisions. Jade and Conner celebrated the catch and they all quickly devoured the fish until only bones were left. Following the meal, Rico took the fish bones and dumped them back in the river, just to be safe.

The group was not only physically worn out but also emotionally drained from the traumatic events of the past twenty-four hours. Rico, Conner, and Jade were very sore and still recovering from their painful injuries. Consequently, the teens made the decision to use the daylight hours to get some rest. They also decided that the one guarding the cave's entrance would do a three-hour shift so they could each get more sleep. This time Savi insisted on being part of the rotation. Because of her injuries, Jade was left out of the mix. Savi volunteered to take the first shift, so the others laid down on the pile of small branches and dying leaves they had placed in the cave and went right to sleep.

After about an hour of keeping watch at the entrance, Savi reached in her vest pocket and pulled out her small Bible. She flipped through the pages until her eyes fell on the words, "Though I walk through the valley of the shadow of death, I will fear no evil for you are with me." She read the words of the Psalm over again and then her eyes filled with tears and she began to cry. Suddenly, she was startled by something rustling in the cave behind her. Instantly, she turned to see Jade walking towards her.

"Gosh, Jade, you scared the heck out of me," Savi whispered in an anxious voice, not wanting to wake Rico and Conner.

"I'm sorry, I sure didn't mean to."

Savi quickly wiped the tears from her face and asked Jade if she was feeling better. Jade confirmed that she was, then leaned toward Savi and studied her face.

"Have you been crying…What's going on?"

"I'm alright, it's nothing," Savi shot back, turning away in embarrassment.

"Savi, what is it?" Jade asked, "and what's that little book in your hand?"

"It's just my Bible," Savi replied.

"Is that what made you cry?"

"No…Well yes, I guess it did."

"What did it say that made you cry?" Jade continued to quiz her with interest.

Savi showed her the words she'd been reading out of Psalm 23 and explained that she wasn't crying because she was sad but because the words brought comfort to her in the midst of her fears. Jade reached over and placed her hand gently on her friend's shoulder and said, "I'm scared too, Savi."

All of a sudden, a rustling noise came from the far side of the clearing. Together they peered out of the cave in the direction of the sound. Then about a hundred feet away inside the tree line, they saw movement. Their hearts raced and Savi felt nervous perspiration begin to form over her lip.

The girls crouched down and slowly lowered their heads. Squinting to see in the direction of the movement, they could barely make out some kind of white spotted brown creature in the woods. Then unexpectedly, a large six-point buck followed by a doe and little fawn emerged from the tree line.

Savi and Jade both let out sighs of relief at the welcome sight. They watched quietly as the family of deer fed on the green grass carpet in the large clearing before them. In the stillness of the early evening, they grazed for a short while, then, led by the buck, they left the clearing with the small fawn trailing behind and reentered the woods. In a matter of seconds, they disappeared just as quickly as they had appeared.

The red-orange sun was now beginning to set and Savi's lookout shift was coming to an end. Jade grabbed a water bottle and the two girls took turns quenching their thirst. Jade then put the bottle down and turned to Savi again and whispered, "How do you know he's really watching over you, Savi?"

"I just believe it," she responded with a sense of assurance.

"Do you think he's watching over me, too?"

Savi smiled. "You can count on it, Jade."

"Does that mean nothing bad is going to happen to us?" Jade asked in a hopeful tone.

"No, Jade. It doesn't mean that at all. It simply means that whatever we face, we don't have to face it alone."

CHAPTER FOURTEEN

The foursome alternated shifts at the cave entrance throughout an uneventful night. At the break of dawn a symphony of assorted birds broke into song signaling the end to Conner's shift and the beginning of a new day.

"Boy, do I feel better," Rico said with a yawn as he stood up and wiped the sleep from his eyes.

"Wish I felt that way," Conner confessed. "My face hurts like crazy and I'm really tired."

"Hey, Sleeping Beauty. Time to get up," Rico announced.

Savi rolled over, opened her eyes and sat up.

"You must be talking to me," she said jokingly to Rico while glancing over at Jade who was just beginning to stir.

Rico rolled his eyes playfully and looked over at Jade who was now listening. "Yeah, I was talking to you. Who else would I be talking to, Conner?"

The morning's lightheartedness brought Jade to her feet smiling and feeling significantly better than the day before. Although everyone was rested, they all woke up hungry. Unfortunately, they had already gone through most of their food supply.

Savi grabbed Rico's fishing gear and started to climb out the cave entrance. "Come on Rico, I'm starving, and it's my turn to catch the fish and your turn to clean 'em."

"Okay, but I've got to do some business in the woods first."

"Great," she shot back while holding her nose.

"Don't you ever have to go?" Rico questioned.

"Yeah, but I don't announce it to the world!" Savi responded.

Rico disappeared behind the cave.

"Hurry up," she needled him. "We're all hungry."

"No peeking," he yelled out.

"Whatever," she fired back.

After Rico had "done his business," the two made their way back to their new favorite fishing spot. Savi reeled in three trout over the course of the next half-hour. Two of them were about one pound each but the last one was bigger, four pounds by Rico's estimate.

Once Rico cleaned the fish, they repeated the same routine from the day before. The two of them proudly brought Savi's cooked catch back to the cave where they all ate with appreciation. After the bones were deposited in the river, they huddled together in the cave to discuss their strategy for the next day.

Sadly, and unbeknownst to the group, just as Rico was returning from depositing the fish bones in the river another rescue raft floated by. Unfortunately, neither of the rescuers in the raft saw the shredded back-pack that Rico had tied to the tree by the river.

By now, the group was convinced that those searching for them probably wouldn't be able to find them. Therefore, they decided to begin the long journey through the wilderness back to Camp Arrowhead. Concerned that bears would surely be feeding close to the river, they made the decision to move about a mile west away from the river and then they would begin to head north.

Savi used the compass from her pack to help guide the group in the right direction. Unfortunately, the only map they had was in Doug's pocket, and it went down the river with him when he was ejected from the raft.

"Savi, how did you learn to use a compass?" Jade asked.

"Since I was young, my dad and I often played a game when we went fishing together. Once we got deep into the woods, he'd give me a map, a compass, and a set of coordinates. Then we'd separate and I'd have to try and find him."

"Weren't you scared, being out there alone?"

"At first I was, but I knew my dad was never more than a few hundred yards away. The game really taught me how to use a map and a compass and I eventually got used to finding my way around the woods alone. It took me a while to get the hang of using them, but now, it's pretty easy for me. Unfortunately, without having a map, the only thing the compass is good for is helping us know the direction we're heading."

"But how do—?"

Rico interrupted Savi and Jade's conversation. "Come on, let's gather up our stuff. We've got a long way to go to get back to Arrowhead and we might as well get started while we still have plenty of daylight."

Within a few minutes, the group assembled their belongings along with Rico and Conner's spears and headed west away from the river. After about a mile they stopped and took a water break.

"By my estimate, it's time to head north. North is that way," Savi said, pointing.

Rico and Conner led out in hope of establishing a good pace. The woods were dense, but they made steady progress.

"Rico, how long do you think it will take us to get back to Camp Arrowhead?" Conner asked.

He mulled the question over then answered, "I'm really not too sure. The camp is probably twenty-five or thirty-miles north of us. Maybe four or five days, depending on what we run into and how many miles we can cover in a day. That's my guess anyway."

"How's your face doing?" Jade asked.

"Probably about the same as your shoulder."

"Not so good then, huh?"

"No, not so good," Conner replied.

"Hey Rico, before you take off…that was a crappy thing I said to you on the football field. I'm really sorry, man…I really am."

"Yeah, you're right it was. But I already thanked you for that, didn't I?"

"You sure did. I think that hit on the football field was worse than the stupid bear's paw!"

"You had it coming…but I do appreciate the apology. How about you keep us on a good pace. I'll go back and check on the girls," Rico concluded.

Savi and Jade were a few yards behind and the brisk pace was demanding on them. Jade could tell that Savi's limp was more pronounced than usual and that she was struggling a bit.

When Jade saw Rico heading toward her, she signaled that she was tired and needed a break. Rico knew he and Conner were tired as well, so they agreed to stop and take a twenty-minute rest.

During the rest stop, both Savi and Jade decided they needed to go relieve themselves in the woods. They took turns keeping watch for each other. Jade went first. When she was done, she came back and told Savi it was her turn. Savi was gone an unusually long time. Jade was just beginning to worry when she heard Savi call her name.

"Jade, come look!" Savi exclaimed. "I found a huckleberry patch. They're all over the place, I saw some birds eating them, so I know they're safe," she added.

In a matter of minutes, they had all stuffed themselves with wild huckleberries. Once they were filled, they took Savi's plastic tarp that she had recovered and filled it up with berries. Then they lifted up all four corners and tied them together with a piece of rope they cut from the coil. All of them looked with glee at their stash knowing they had enough to feed themselves for at least a couple of days.

Now sporting purple hands and lips from the berries, the group was revived. They packed up and began again making their way north toward Camp Arrowhead. The foursome had covered about three miles when they realized they needed to think about finding a place to sleep for the night. As they moved through the woods, they came upon a small stream about three feet wide and used it to quench their thirst and refill their nearly empty water bottles.

"I never knew I'd be so happy to see water," Jade said after she took a sip from her canteen.

"It's always just there when you turn on the tap," Rico added.

Savi looked around at their surroundings and then theorized, "I think there's a lot of things we take for granted. Things we always just expect to be there. Like food and water."

"If we get out of this, I don't think I'll ever look at a water faucet the same," Jade admitted.

Conner was just about to chime in, when Savi interrupted him. "Shhh," she whispered. "Don't move."

Everyone looked at Savi. For reasons unknown something had shaken her. She stood in place, staring at something in the bushes about thirty feet across the stream.

"Savi, what is it?" Jade whispered.

"Turn slowly and you'll see!" Savi replied.

CHAPTER FIFTEEN

J ust as she had asked, the others turned slowly to see what had brought about the terrified look on Savi's face. Instantly, they understood why she appeared so frightened. Across the stream next to a cluster of bushes loomed a very large, dirty gray wolf. There was no doubt about its identity. It stood still and glared at the horrified foursome. For the first few moments, none of them were sure of what to do next. Then the situation went from bad to worse.

A second gray wolf emerged from the same cluster of bushes. This one began snarling and bearing his teeth, which incited the first wolf to do the same. Instinctively, everyone realized that the wolves were preparing to attack.

"Okay, slowly," Rico whispered. "Everybody stand up and take out your knives. Conner, you start moving upstream with Jade. Savi, you follow close behind her. I'll bring up the rear. Conner, listen…no sudden moves or running…but go quickly!"

Conner did as instructed and the four moved in unison in a tight-knit formation up the right side of the stream. Both Conner and Rico had spears in hand ready to defend themselves and the group at a moment's notice. The girls likewise had their pocketknives out, knowing they would use them as a last resort.

Instead of charging across the stream, the wolves began moving up the left bank, mimicking the group's movements. When they didn't think it could get any worse, two more wolves came out of the same cluster of bushes and joined the others. Now there were four hideous looking creatures stalking them from across the stream. The wolves seemed content to bide their time and wait for the right moment to strike.

After traveling cautiously but deliberately upstream for about a hundred yards, the group began hearing the roar of crashing waters. It sounded very different from the rapids on the river, so they weren't sure what they were actually hearing. The further they moved upstream the louder the noise grew.

At the same time, they noticed that the stream was widening, adding distance between them and the predators on the opposite bank. When the watercourse turned slightly to the left, they finally saw the source of the roar they'd been hearing. It was a beautiful waterfall with a huge circular pool in front of it measuring a hundred feet in diameter. Behind the majestic falls was a large flat rock ledge that served as a floor leading into a deep cave behind it.

Across the stream, the wolves kept their eyes trained on the group. The predators moved deliberately and in sync up the bank, mirroring the teens every step.

"Listen, if we can get behind the waterfall onto that rock ledge, it'll be almost impossible for the wolves to get to us," Rico yelled over the crashing waters. He turned toward Conner. "Take Jade and Savi and climb on those rocks and make your way across the pool to the ledge behind the falls. I'll follow you once you're about halfway to the ledge. Now hurry."

Conner led Jade and Savi across the rocks that jutted out of the pool in front of the ledge. In the process of navigating their way over the tops of the rocks, Savi slipped and fell into the cold pool near the front of the falls. She let out a scream as the chill of the water shot through her body, but she quickly recovered and climbed back onto the rock and continued on.

Eventually, Conner, Savi, and Jade made their way behind the falls and stood on the flat ledge. Conner peered around the cascading water to see how Rico was progressing.

When Rico saw that the others were about halfway to the ledge, he began making his way up the shore instead of over the rocks. The wolves appeared disturbed by this new development and showed it by moving closer to the shore on the other side of the pool. As they did, they snarled viciously and again showed their frightening teeth. Acting more agitated than before, they looked at Rico moving up the bank alone and then surveyed the ledge and rocks in front of it, where the others were now standing. You could almost see the wheels turning in the wolves' heads as they tried to figure out how to gain access to their prey. One wolf began climbing around the back of the waterfall looking for a way to the other side. The other wolves eagerly followed its lead.

Rico chose to take a different route than the others to get behind the falls. Along the shore were two large pine trees he had to go around to get close to the rocks directly in front of the falls. As he came around the first tree, he accidentally dropped his spear and it banged against a rock. All at once, he heard a strange buzzing noise above him. As he looked up into the tree, his eyes fell on a large mud hive with bees furiously darting in and about it. He quickly picked up his spear and started to run. Suddenly, wasps were everywhere around Rico, stinging him on his neck, arms, and hands. The pain of multiple stings tore through his body as the angry wasps attacked him relentlessly.

Desperate, Rico dove into the cold water in front of the waterfall. He swam under the falls to where the others were standing, leaving his spear floating behind. The others grabbed him and helped pull him up onto the rock ledge. Knowing the importance of the weapon, Savi leaned forward and grabbed Rico's spear from the water as it drifted toward the ledge.

Unexpectedly, the wolves arrived close to where Rico had just dived into the pool. The wasps swarmed around them as well, but the bees only seemed to be an annoyance to them. The wolves moved away from the tree and again peered back at the shivering teens behind the cascading water.

Rico was hurting badly from the numerous wasp stings, and Savi and Jade were busy pulling out the stingers still imbedded in the swollen wounds. While the girls attended to Rico, Conner kept his eyes on the wolves and guarded the front of the cave.

When it seemed like the wolves had no way of making it across the water, one of the them leapt onto a rock and then jumped onto another rock, trying to get closer to the big ledge where the four were gathered. The lone wolf, who appeared to be the leader of the pack, snarled and growled from the rock about ten feet away.

Conner stood facing his determined opponent with his spear tip pointed directly at it. The beast growled and snarled at him, but kept its place. When the angry wolf realized the distance between them was too far to jump, it plunged into the water and began swimming toward the ledge.

"Savi, I need your help now!" Conner yelled frantically. Instantly, Savi grabbed Rico's spear and positioned herself next to Conner. When the determined wolf reached the ledge, clawing it with his paw, Conner and Savi plunged their spears into its neck from opposite sides. The wolf recoiled and fell backwards into the water bleeding and yelping. Somehow, the wounded animal made its way across the pool to the water's edge. It hobbled out of the water and collapsed bleeding onto the bank.

Conner turned to Savi. "Wow, that was close. Did you know wolves could swim?"

"I've never thought about it till now. But I guess if dogs can swim, why not wolves?" she replied.

"What should we do about the wolf? If Vexel smells its blood, we're done," Conner warned Savi.

Savi looked over at the wolf they had speared and saw him mortally wounded but still twitching on the shore.

"There's really nothing we can do at this point. Let's hope it crawls away. I've been watching and at least one other wolf is still lurking around in the woods over there."

Despite the danger, Conner was unwilling to let the wounded wolf lie bloodied on the bank and do nothing about it.

"If I don't do something about that wolf, we might as well put out a welcome mat for Vexel. We've got to at least get it in the pool, so the water can dilute the smell of the blood."

"Conner, no way are you going over there," Savi insisted.

"I thought that's what you'd say."

Without warning Conner dove into the pool and headed toward the wolf.

"Conner!" Savi screamed.

He swam to the shore, pulled out his knife and cautiously approached the dying wolf. When he reached the wolf, he used his knife to put it out of its misery. He then grabbed the hind feet of the dead animal and dragged it into the pool. He pulled the carcass through the water about twenty feet to a set of rocks and wedged it in between them, so it wouldn't drift away. Exhausted, he clung to a rock and took a minute to catch his breath. After doing so, he returned to the ledge behind the falls.

"I can't believe you just did that, Conner. What if the wolves attacked you?" Savi questioned in protest.

Dripping wet Conner glared back at her. "Calm down, Savi. It had to be done. We've already got enough trouble without inviting Vexel over for dinner. I did what I had to do."

Savi replied in an apologetic tone. "I'm sorry, Conner. I just didn't want to see you get hurt or worse. I know you did what you thought best."

"I get it. We're all under a lot of stress out here. With Rico down, it's my turn to be responsible and man up," he concluded.

The sun fell below the trees, and it was almost dark. Now that everyone realized the wolves could swim, there was more concern than ever about the rest of the pack still prowling the area. Consequently, they decided to post two guards at a time all night long. They stationed a guard with a spear on each side of the ledge behind the waterfall. Rico was still hurting. But he recovered noticeably as the evening wore on.

Savi had fallen into the pool and now that the sun was down, she shivered visibly. She retrieved her life vest that she'd previously hooked on Rico's backpack and draped it over her shoulders like a jacket. Sadly, now only Rico and Jade had backpacks, though they too had been damaged somewhat by the bear. Since Jade was still feeling the effects of her river accident, Savi and Conner agreed to rotate carrying her backpack until she recovered fully.

While keeping an eye out for the wolves, everyone ate their fill of huckleberries and drank from the falls, which rehydrated them. Once they were all full, Rico and Jade took the first three-hour shift of guard duty. They alternated using Savi's small flashlight to keep a lookout for the lurking wolves. This time Jade felt well enough to participate in the rotation, which helped everyone to get some much-needed rest.

The long damp night behind the falls was accompanied by the occasional haunting sounds of wolves howling into the moonless sky. Though they made no attempt to scale the ledge that night, everyone realized the predators were still close by and as always, on the hunt.

After a tense night, the morning sun shimmered through the falls and created a beautiful rainbow in the mist. In the sunlight, they saw that the wolf Conner wedged between the rocks was still there. The other wolves were nowhere to be found.

The chilled teens welcomed the growing warmth ushered in by the new day. After eating a few handfuls of berries for breakfast and drinking some water, they refilled their canteens and water bottles from the falling water and sat down together to discuss what they should do next.

"We've got to keep moving north," Rico began.

"What about the wolves?" Jade replied with concern.

"We'll deal with them if we have to," Rico interjected. "But we just can't stay here much longer. There's too much blood around and we're already running low on food. As much as I hate to say it, there's no alternative but to take our chances out there."

"I agree," Savi broke in. "We've got to keep heading north toward the camp. The compass says we should go that way." She pointed past the waterfall.

"Hey, I need to say something I hope doesn't offend anyone before we go. I know the water is cold but we all smell really bad. And we need to clean up a bit. Especially you, Rico," Savi added.

"Gee thanks, Savi. Are you saying I stink? Nice…I was just in the water yesterday," Rico shot back.

"Well, it wasn't long enough. You do smell pretty bad, Rico," Jade confirmed.

"Oh great, now everybody thinks I stink. For your information, I've been paddling down a river, cleaning fish, fighting bears, hiking for miles, and putting up with you guys for the past two days. I have a right to stink," Rico blurted out.

"Wow, Mister Overreaction, I'm just suggesting you take a bath," Savi said in a mocking tone.

Once Rico and Conner surveyed the area to ensure no wolves were around, they appeased the girls and jumped into the chilly pool.

"Hey, girls. Anyone have some perfume I can borrow?" Rico joked.

"Yeah," Savi replied. "I've got some. It's called deodorant."

Rico filled his mouth with water and tried to spit it at her. "Very funny, Savi."

After a couple of minutes, the guys got out and then the girls followed suit. Savi and Jade played in the water as if they were two kids on vacation at a resort. Their laughter and giggles echoed through the trees, which caused Rico to scold them to keep it down. By this time, the sun beat down above them. The girls decided to lie down on one of the rocks in front of the falls for a few minutes. The full sun would hasten the time it took for them to dry off.

Suddenly, the wolves appeared out of nowhere, just a short leap from the unsuspecting girls. Apparently, they had secretly crossed back over from the other side of the pool and were lurking in the woods waiting for an opportunity. Now the wolves subtly inched forward, hoping to catch their prey by surprise.

Rico was the first to spot them. He picked up his spear, jumped back into the water and started desperately working his way toward the girls.

"Savi! Jade! Look out!" he shouted. Just then, one of the wolves readied itself to lunge at the defenseless girls.

Conner grabbed his spear and followed Rico, both now racing to save Savi and Jade. Despite their best efforts, they couldn't get there in time. The closest wolf sprang into the air and landed on the far side of the rock where the girls were sitting. They both screamed and froze in fear not knowing what to do next. Just then, another wolf leaped onto a rock close to Rico and Conner. They were now surrounded and in a hopeless situation.

Suddenly, the distinct crack of a rifle shot rang out and the wolf that was near the girls immediately fell off the rock and floated motionless in the water.

Everyone was so overwhelmed that they froze in place. Another three shots were fired in rapid succession and instantly the wolf by Rico and Conner went down as well. Startled by the gunfire, the final wolf beat a hasty retreat into the woods and disappeared into the dense foliage.

"What just happened, Savi?" a stunned Jade asked after she collapsed back onto the rock.

"Somebody just saved our lives," Savi answered.

"Are you guys okay?" Rico and Conner asked once they reached the rock where Savi and Jade were sitting in shock.

"Yeah, we're all right," Savi replied with a strong sigh. "But who in the world shot the wolves?"

Rico looked across the pool and noticed a lone dark figure wearing a camouflaged bush hat walking toward them. He carried a huge backpack and toted a scoped rifle on his shoulder. Pointing toward the mystery man who was approaching, Rico finally answered Savi's question. "I'm guessing it was him."

CHAPTER SIXTEEN

The astonished group made it to shore as quickly as they could. Once there, they came upon the bloody carcass of the second wolf the stranger had killed. It had been shot in the head and must have died instantly. The bullet had entered the wolf's head cleanly on one side, but it blew the other half of its face away.

Everyone was a bit apprehensive as the young, tall, and rugged looking black man got closer to the group on the shore. He walked up to them slowly and confidently extending his right hand first to Rico.

"I'm Luke." Rico did not respond at first. He kept his place studying the young man, not sure if he could really trust him. "You don't have to worry. I'm a friend."

What he said appeared to put Rico at ease. "My name's Rico," he finally replied, taking the man's hand and shaking it.

"Pleased to meet you, Rico."

"Hi Luke, I'm Savi, and this is Jade," she said pointing at her friend.

"Glad to meet you girls," Luke said warmly. "And who might you be?"

"Hey Luke, I'm Conner." They shook hands with each other.

"Now, what in the world are you all doing out here in these parts?" Luke asked them.

"We had a rafting accident and lost our guide," Rico answered for the group. "We're trying to make our way back to Camp Arrowhead."

"Well you're heading in the right direction...but you've probably got over twenty miles to go. And, I might add, over some pretty rough terrain."

"Do you have a cell phone on you?" Conner asked.

"Cell phone? What would I do with a cell phone out here? There's no service for miles, not until you get to Arrowhead anyway, and even then it's spotty at best."

"Is there *anything* around here?" Jade asked. "Someone that might help us get back or a place we can get some food?"

"What are you looking for, a *Burger King*?" Luke said jokingly.

"No, of course not. I was thinking of a town or house between here and Arrowhead. Maybe even a ranger station."

Luke shook his head. "I'm afraid you're out of luck, angel. There's really nothing or nobody out here. I mean, no one that you'd want to meet anyway. As a matter of fact, looks like you've already met some of the locals," Luke noted while staring at Conner's bandaged face.

"Where do you live, Luke?" Savi asked.

"About thirty miles southwest of here. After our place, the next cabin is straight south about ten miles. The closest town to our cabin is twenty miles away."

Savi stepped closer toward Luke and gently grabbed his hand. "Let me be the first to thank you for saving our lives, Luke. You're quite a shot with that thing." She glanced at the rifle on his shoulder. "So, why are you out here alone so far from your home? Are you hunting?"

Luke's face tightened and he became noticeably tense. Then collecting himself, he finally answered, "Yep, that's what I'm doing out here. I'm hunting."

The way he answered the question made Rico feel a bit uneasy. Something disturbed him but he couldn't put his finger on why. "Are you hunting for wolves?" he inquired.

Luke paused then he continued. "Nope, I'm hunting for Vexel."

It was as if all of them had seen a ghost at the same time. Savi looked at Rico, who turned to Jade, who then glanced at Conner. All four of them thought the same thing, but Jade broke the silence. "Vexel...you mean he's...real?"

"Oh yeah. He's real."

Rico felt the hairs at the base of his neck rise at his answer.

"How do you know that?" Jade asked.

"Because he killed someone I loved three years ago," Luke replied in a sullen tone.

"Oh Luke, I'm so sorry," Jade said. The others silently echoed her sentiments with sympathetic nods.

"How did it happen?" Savi asked.

For the next hour, Luke told them all about Vexel, including how the mysterious beast had tracked down and killed his father during a hunting trip.

"That evil beast completely devoured my father's flesh until basically all that was left were his bones." He also told them about the promise he made standing over his father's grave three years earlier. He vowed that one-day, he'd hunt down and kill Vexel or he'd die trying. Not only to avenge his father's death, but to rid the earth of the hideous creature. He was seventeen years old then, but now he was twenty, and still had not fulfilled his vow.

"Two weeks ago, I started looking for him again. I finally picked up his trail about four days ago. And I've been tracking him ever since. That is until I came upon you all last evening."

"How did you find us?" Rico asked.

"Between the four of you, you were making enough noise to raise the dead," Luke replied half-joking.

"You mean you've been here all night?" Conner asked.

"Yep."

"Why didn't you let us know you were around last night?"

"No need to. You all were doing just fine by yourselves. But today was different. I could tell you needed a little assistance."

"If it weren't for you, we'd probably all be dead now and never heard from again."

Luke accepted the compliment but then his face became taut. "Now listen up, I'm going to give you a few things to take with you and some words of advice. Then I'll send you on your way, and I'll get back to tracking and hopefully killing Vexel...Who among you has used a pistol before?" Luke asked.

Both Savi and Rico raised their hands.

"No offense, Missy, but I think I'll give this to Rico." He handed him a small caliber pistol. "But use it wisely since it's only a six shooter. After that it's just a hammer," he said with grin.

"Savi, here's an old map. It's pretty beat up, but it might help. I see you've already got yourself a compass...Know how to use it?"

"She sure does," Jade bragged about her friend.

Luke then gave them some dried fruit and deer jerky. It looked like enough to last them a couple of days. He also traced out on the old map what he thought was the best way to get back to Arrowhead. Just as Luke said, it would be a difficult trip. The group learned they'd have to cross a mountain range to get back to the camp. He also pointed out some camping spots along the way and a hidden cave in the mountains that would serve them well as a final night's camping stop should they need it. Lastly, he cautioned them about snakes.

"There are lots of harmless ones around these parts. Those you don't have to worry about. It's the others that are a problem. Just be sure you steer clear of the rattlesnakes. A single bite can kill a person. One species is called the Great Basin Rattlesnake and the other is known as the Northern Pacific Rattlesnake. The only thing you have going in your favor is that they're not naturally aggressive, unless of course they're cornered, stepped on, or taken by surprise. Just keep your eyes open is all I'm saying."

Before Luke left and sent the teens on their way, he pointed out the last natural obstacle they would have to cross to get back to the Camp. It was a river about a quarter mile wide called the Susquehanna.

He went on to say that every year on September 1, just five days away, the Clayton Dam is opened for fourteen days. He informed them that once the dam opened, the river was virtually impassible. Then Luke finished by warning them that if they didn't make it across the Susquehanna River by August 31, they would be stuck on the wrong side of the river for at least another two weeks.

Luke looked at each of them one last time and shook hands with Rico and Conner, who in turn thanked him for everything. Both girls likewise gave him warm farewell hugs and echoed their thanks again as well. They all watched and waved a heartfelt good-bye as Luke disappeared into the trees on a mission he was committed to finish. Obsessed by his desire to kill Vexel, he was compelled to leave the struggling teens to make it on their own. He wondered if their paths would cross again.

Luke had deliberately withheld one vital piece of information from them during his visit. He decided it was best not to tell them this one thing since it would only increase their already high level of tension. Vexel was in the area and he too was moving north.

CHAPTER SEVENTEEN

They all drank freely from the waterfall and filled their canteens and water bottles before leaving. They also ate some of the deer jerky that Luke had given them and finished the last of the huckleberries. By this time it was early afternoon and they needed to travel another four miles through dense forest and heavy underbrush to get to the destination that Luke had recommended.

During their time together, Luke was kind enough to map out a specific route, coupled with a timetable that would get the group to the Susquehanna River by the afternoon of August 30, a full day before the Clayton Dam would open and make the river impassible. The plan required that they move at a reasonable pace and cover about five miles a day. Luke cautioned them that the last day would be much more difficult and slower because they would have to cross over a mountain range. This was the last major obstacle before they'd reach the Susquehanna River.

Traveling through the dense forest was tough enough, but the heavy underbrush made it even more difficult. Approximately every half-mile everyone got so exhausted that they had to stop and rest. Savi was quick to inform the others that they were already falling behind the predetermined timetable. But she also realized that there wasn't much they could do about it since they were clearly giving it their all.

The afternoon dragged on while the group navigated its way through the thick and tricky wilderness. By late afternoon, they estimated that they had somewhere around a half mile to go before reaching their destination.

Exhausted, Jade looked at Savi and asked, "Can't we just camp here for the night? I don't think I can go any farther."

"We're getting close, Jade. Just push yourself. We'll be there soon."

"I can't go on. I need a break," she insisted.

Jade's exposed arms and legs were bleeding from scratches she received from the dense underbrush. Seeing that she was thoroughly spent, Savi called ahead to Rico, who was walking the point position.

"We need to stop for a couple minutes," Savi declared. "Just a short break, and then we can get back at it."

Rico looked up at the canopy of trees above. "It'll be dark soon." He shook his head. "No, we've got to keep moving and make every use of daylight. It's just a little further on, then we'll stop."

"That's not happening without a few minutes break," she shot back.

Savi stopped and sat down ... then watched as Jade crumbled to the ground and let out a huge sigh of relief.

Savi graciously reached over and handed Jade her canteen filled with water and a piece of dried fruit.

Tired but grateful, Jade looked over at her friend. "Thanks, Savi. I'm really trying to keep up. I don't know how you're doing it with your foot and everything."

"I'm struggling too, but we've only got a little ways to go before we can rest for the night."

Frustrated, Rico walked a few yards back to where Savi and Jade rested and roused them firmly. "Girls, it's time! We've got to go before it's too dark to travel. Come on, we're almost there."

Savi got up like a woman four times her age. Once she did, she reached her hand out to Jade. "Come on, Cinderella," she said with a big smile. "You've got to get up before your carriage turns into a pumpkin."

Jade grabbed Savi's outstretched hands, and with her friend's help, got to her feet. "What I really need are some ruby slippers like Dorothy had in the *Wizard of Oz*. I'd click my heels together and say, 'There's no place like home. There's no place like home,'" Jade joked as she started walking again.

As they pushed through the final leg of the day's journey, Jade looked over at Savi and told her, "Actually, as bad as this place is, it's better than being at home. I feel that way because you're here, Savi…I think you're one of the best friends I've ever had."

"What about me? Do you love me too?" Conner asked Jade from behind in a mocking voice.

"Shut up, Conner!" Jade snarled. "And what are you doing eavesdropping on our conversation anyway?"

"I'm just trying to learn a bit more about my new girlfriend!" he answered in a playful tone.

"Dream on, lover boy," she fired back.

The group fell into an extended period of silence. They trekked their way through the darkening forest one difficult step at a time. Although the going was slow, they finally arrived at their destination. When they got there, Savi walked over to Jade, who had already found a large rock and was sitting with her back against it. She put her hand on her shoulder and gave it a good squeeze, congratulating her for pushing through her pain and fatigue to complete the day's journey.

"Jade, I heard what you said back there. And I'm really happy that you feel that way. Although we just met, I think of you as a great friend already. I'll bet we'll be friends for the rest of our lives," Savi added in a hopeful tone.

"That would be awesome," Jade replied.

Luke had picked a great overnight spot for the group, on top of a relatively secure hilltop. It was about forty feet high with steep rock walls on all sides. The natural outcropping, thousands of years in the making, was practically vertical on every side. That made it almost impossible for predators to climb up and surprise them. Yet the narrow goat trail that zigzagged up one of the sides made it just accessible enough for the tired hikers to summit the rocky rise.

From their elevated vantage point, their view was unobstructed for about a quarter mile in all directions. The night was cooler than usual as a result of a cold breeze that blew in from the north. Though none of them were experts in air pressure or cloud patterns, they agreed it could indicate a possible change in the weather. Or worse yet, a storm was coming.

Once the group settled in and had a chance to recuperate, they rehydrated themselves and ate some more of the food that Luke gave them earlier in the day. Conner and Rico went back down the goat trail to gather sticks and small branches to build a fire. Once they returned and lit the fire, the teens surrounded it and gradually began to thaw. At first, they sat quietly and relished the warmth and a momentary sense of safety. Then Jade broke the silence.

"Do you think we'll make it to the river by the last day of August?"

"Yeah, I think so," Conner interjected. "But we're going to have to keep pressing on. Tomorrow will be another tough day, so we'd better get some rest."

"I'm thinking we only need one guard per shift tonight. Let's make the rotation three hours long. Is everybody good with that?" Rico asked. Then he added, "How about if I take the first shift?"

Everyone nodded in relief and lay down by the fire to sleep.

Rico began his vigil and walked slowly around the approximately fifty foot oblong hilltop. As the moon slipped behind a gathering of ominous looking clouds, the visibility decreased noticeably. In the distance, Rico saw a flash of lightning illuminate the night sky for an instant, followed by a loud thunderclap several seconds later. It was now apparent that some really bad weather was approaching their exposed position.

Rico found an open spot near the fire and sat down. Though it was mostly embers now, the warmth it radiated felt good. Not far away, Conner snored softly. He checked on the girls, who lay side-by-side to best preserve their body heat. They were also asleep. The rocky hilltop didn't provide much in terms of creature comforts, but at least they felt safe.

His moment of solitude was short-lived. In the distance, what sounded like an airplane slowly filled his ears. It appeared to be flying relatively low and moved quickly toward their position. This, he concluded, meant that it was a nighttime search plane looking for the lost rafters. In just a few moments, it was within sight and flying very low, no more than a thousand feet, Rico guessed.

Instantly, he dropped his spear and attempted to pull the lighter out of his vest pocket to try and signal the plane. Then he remembered that after lighting the fire, he had given it back to Savi. The plane was now directly overhead and Rico waved frantically to get the pilot's attention, but standing on the dark hilltop he went unnoticed.

Slowly and steadily, the plane flew out of sight. Rico kicked himself for giving Savi back her lighter instead of holding on to it and for forgetting to ask her for her little flashlight before she lay down. He was now becoming convinced that rescue was no longer an option. The group would have to get to the river without delay by August 31, or else. He was confident they could do that if they stayed on pace. But nothing could prepare them for what tomorrow would bring!

CHAPTER EIGHTEEN

All was quiet for the remainder of Rico's shift following the airplane incident. Knowing that Jade was next in line for guard duty, he had intentionally extended his shift an extra hour. He chose to do this so she could enjoy some much-needed additional rest. But after being on watch for four hours, he was tired and decided the time had come to wake her.

Rico gave Jade several gentle nudges before her eyes finally opened. She let out a yawn, uncertain where she was at first. It took her a few minutes before she was fully awake. She strolled over, rubbing sleep from her eyes.

"Thanks for getting me up," she said after another yawn. "I'm sure you're ready for a few hours sleep."

Rico looked at Jade and saw that her beautiful face glowed, even on the moonless night. She looked back at him with a girlish smile and surveyed his handsome features. He caught her staring at him and felt a bit embarrassed.

"What? Why are you looking at me that way?" he asked, defensively.

"Oh, now I can't look at you without your permission," she shot back.

"No. I'm not saying that," he added while doing his best to mask his embarrassment.

"Then what are you saying? Either you like or don't like the way I'm looking at you...Which is it?" Jade pressed him.

Rico knew he was on the spot. Jade stood directly in front of him waiting for an answer.

She raised an eyebrow, smiled and asked him again. "Well? Which is it?"

Before she knew what had happened, Rico reached out and grabbed her, pulled her close and kissed her firmly on the lips. Jade's first instinct was to pull away, but instead, she melted into his strong arms. At first, he squeezed her so hard that she nearly lost her breath. Following the welcome kiss, she placed her head gently on his shoulder and they hugged for what seemed like minutes. Then, Rico pulled his head back a bit. When Jade took her head off his shoulder to look squarely at him, he kissed her again, this time softly.

"Do I stink now?" he asked with a wry smile.

"Yeah, just a little," she replied jokingly.

"I can't believe you just said that," Rico added playfully.

Jade looked at him affectionately but gently scolded, "There's probably a big brown bear or maybe even Vexel climbing up the side of this hill right now. And I'm standing here kissing you...I'm supposed to be on guard duty."

"You're right. We shouldn't have done that," Rico said, while pretending to be serious.

"I didn't mean…" Jade started to say.

"Good night, soldier. We're counting on you to defend the fort. Don't let us down," Rico said as he walked away.

Jade stood alone looking out over the night's dark expanse. For the first time she thought she understood what it might feel like to be in love. Though it had been about two years since a boy had kissed her for the first time, from this night on she would always consider Rico's kiss to be her first.

For the rest of her shift, she thought about the precious minutes spent alone with Rico. She wondered how in the world she'd so quickly and easily been swept off of her feet.

Jade woke up Conner quietly and whispered to him that it was time for his shift to begin. When he had collected himself and walked over to Jade, he asked her if she was interested in walking and talking with him a bit. To his dismay, she declined, claiming she was tired. In actuality, she was wide-awake and still captivated by the tender moments she and Rico shared together. Her heart and mind raced in such a way that she was concerned she wouldn't be able to sleep. But shortly after she lay down, her eyelids grew heavy and she fell fast asleep.

Standing guard alone on the hilltop that dark and breezy night, Conner felt lonely. This was an emotion he had not allowed himself to feel for years. Quite the contrary, he learned to distance himself from his deep-seated feelings of abandonment. Instead, he covered them up with a masterful show of bravado or with lots of friends and social activities. Now, the pain of his facial wound, the stress associated with the current situation, and an overwhelming sense of loneliness all combined to bring him to tears.

Alone in the dark, Conner sobbed quietly for nearly an hour.

The night shift was long but eventually it was over and he woke Savi to take his place. Immediately, she could tell something was wrong. Conner's usual cocky stride and disposition were missing. He appeared sullen and troubled like she'd never seen him before.

"What's up, Conner?" Savi asked in a friendly tone.

"Not much, I think I'm just tired and…and I'm not sure what else," he mumbled.

"That's easy to understand. It's been a rough few days."

"It's not about being out here, Savi…" Then he hesitated a moment and seemed to catch himself. "Oh, just what you need, to listen to my problems, huh?"

"Sometimes talking about things helps," Savi offered.

"I guess that's true, but I'm not good at trusting," he confided. "Seems like every time I trust someone, I end up hurt or alone."

"Maybe you're trusting the wrong people."

"What do you mean by that?" Conner asked annoyed.

"Just what I said," Savi repeated. "Maybe you're not trusting the right people."

"So how do you know who to trust…and who not to trust?"

"I look at what people do, not just at what they say."

"Like how?" he asked.

Savi thought for a moment, then said, "Let me answer your question with a question. Suppose somebody told you that they were honest, but you consistently caught them lying, what would you think?"

"I'd think they were really a liar. Even though they said they were honest."

Savi nodded. "I totally agree. So, the bottom line is that I've learned to trust people more based on what they do, than on what they say."

"That makes a lot of sense," Conner admitted.

Savi stepped forward, wrapped her arms around Conner and gave him a big hug. Rising up on her tiptoes, she whispered in his ear, "I'm glad you feel that way." Then she looked down at Conner's watch. "It's late. You'd better get some sleep. We'll be leaving in a couple hours from now and you need some rest."

"Savi, I don't usually tell people this kind of stuff… Don't tell the others what we've talked about, okay?"

"Shucks, Conner, I was just going to wake those guys up and tell 'em everything," Savi said with a big smile. "Now go. Get some sleep."

"Good night, Savi. You're pretty smart for a little squirt," Conner said jokingly, leaving them both smiling as he walked away.

There would be no majestic sunrise on this day due to the dark gray clouds hiding the normally blue morning sky. All at once, a few raindrops started to fall. Then the rain fell so hard that it pelted the faces of those still sleeping and woke them up. Before long, everyone was stirring and making preparation for the day's march ahead.

When Jade saw Rico, she greeted him with a girl-ish smile and went on about her business as if nothing had happened the night before. Rico acknowledged her with a raised eyebrow and returned the friendly greet-ing. He then proceeded to carry on like his ordinary self. They both were doing a good job of pretending things were normal, except occasionally when they would catch each other sneaking a look.

After breakfast, the group decided to sit down and look at the map with the route penned by Luke the day before. Since the map was tucked away in Rico's backpack a short distance away from where they were sitting, Savi got up and went over to retrieve it. Her head turned back over her shoulder when Jade laughed at something. Not seeing where she was going, Savi accidentally stumbled into Rico's pack that was leaning up against a rock.

Instantly, she heard it, a loud rattling sound and then a warning from Rico. "Savi, stop! Just stand per-fectly still!"

Confused by the warning to Savi, Jade looked around to see what was the matter. Her eyes quickly focused on something moving next to Savi's pack. She then real-ized what she was looking at and let out a blood-cur-dling shriek. The scream caused Savi to flinch, alarming the rattlesnake coiled up next to her.

Before Savi had time to react, the snake sprang at her and clamped its venomous fangs through her poly-propylene wetsuit pants and into the calf of her right leg. Instantly, Savi crumpled to the ground writhing in pain with the snake still clinging to her leg.

Jumping into to action, Rico hit the snake with his spear and knocked it off of her. Then he pulled out the pistol Luke had given him and deposited three bullets into the rattler, killing it instantly, though it continued to squirm for the next few seconds.

Conner ran to help Savi. She held her calf, wailed loudly and rolled on the ground in severe pain. Conner bent down and pulled up Savi's wetsuit past the wound. Then he put his mouth over the snakebite and began sucking the poison out as hard as he could. All through this painful process Savi continued to scream frantically. Every couple of seconds, he spit the venom out of his mouth and then repeated the same procedure.

Savi became quiet and started to shake. Jade sat down close and cradled her head in the crook of her arm. She did her best to comfort her friend but also feared she might be dying.

"Savi," Jade pleaded, "come on, stay with us."

Rico quickly whipped off his belt and used it to tie a tourniquet on Savi's upper right leg. Pulling out his knife, he cut a straight incision between the two fang marks, which caused the immediate flow of blood. Savi screamed loudly and tried to pull away but her strength faded. Rico, following Conner's lead, then sucked more of the venom and blood out of the wound. Conner disinfected the spot where Rico made his incision and then carefully bandaged the snakebite.

Feeling distraught, Jade turned to Rico and Conner with tears streaming down her face and asked them in an anxious whisper, "Do you think she's going die?"

Conner and Rico looked at one another and back at Jade. Then Rico spoke for the two of them.

"We really don't know!"

CHAPTER NINETEEN

Savi slipped in and out of consciousness. From time to time, she twitched and shook uncontrollably. Jade had planted herself by Savi's side and monitored her every move. Savi's breathing was slow and her pulse hard to detect, but she was alive and that's all that mattered for now.

Rico and Conner looked at one another, nodded, and quietly went to the far side of the hilltop.

"She's too sick to move anywhere," Rico said after he made sure they were out of earshot. "We're going to have to stay here at least another day."

"I agree," Conner replied. "Is there anything else we can do for her?"

"We've got to keep releasing the pressure on the tourniquet about every ten minutes for the next couple hours. It may lessen the amount of toxin that travels through her body. Besides that, I can't think of anything else to do, except to try and keep her warm."

Jade began to sob as she looked down at her friend's motionless body. Even the slightest movement or sound from Savi helped Jade retain a sense of hope that she might recover.

At a loss as to how to help Savi, Jade sat silently gazing at the first girlfriend she had ever really trusted. There was something about Savi that was pure and wholesome, yet at the same time, she was feisty and fun. She seemed confident but had a humility about her that made her endearing. She read the Bible but never sounded preachy or judgmental. She lived her faith, instead of just talked about it.

All at once, Savi began shaking and let out a horrific scream.

"Savi! Can you hear me? It's Jade! You're going to be okay…just hang on!"

The shaking slowed and then eventually stopped. In a matter of seconds, she fell motionless again.

Jade noticed the top of Savi's little book peeking out from her front vest pocket. She reached across her stationary body and took it out. She still remembered the words Savi had read to her and started thumbing through the book searching for something called Psalm 23. Somewhere close to the middle of the book she found it.

Rico and Conner were talking privately a few feet away from the girls. When they finished, they came back and sat down next to her.

"How are you doing, Jade?" Rico asked, placing his hand softly on hers.

"I'm afraid she's going to die, no matter what we do," she said sadly.

Rico looked at Jade sympathetically and then admitted, "There's a lot of things in life we can't control, Jade, and this is one of them."

"Maybe that's why she was reading it," Jade said.

"What are you talking about?" Conner asked.

"Savi was reading from this book the other day. I asked her what she was reading and she showed it to me. It's funny, but something about the words touched me in a way I can't really describe," Jade said in a reflective tone.

"What did it say?" Conner asked.

"I don't remember exactly. That's why I want to read it again," Jade replied.

"I'd like to hear what you're talking about…Will you read it out loud?" Conner asked.

"I guess so," she said.

Jade glanced over at Rico. "Do you mind?"

"No, I don't care, read it."

Jade brought the small brown book up close and began reading the words Savi had read to her. "Even though I walk through the valley of the shadow of death, I will fear no evil, for he is with me."

Jade then lowered the book along with her head and immediately started to sob. Rico and Conner both placed a hand on her back. After Jade stopped crying, the three of them sat for the longest time in silence staring down at Savi. Now lying still before them, she was quietly fighting the biggest battle of her young life.

It was late afternoon and Jade hadn't moved from her friend's side since she was bitten. Rico and Conner edged a few feet away again and talked in hushed tones. When they were done, the boys walked back over to Jade and told her she needed to take a break. They offered her some water and a portion of the remaining dried fruit and jerky that Luke had given them. At first, she resisted, but finally she realized a short break and having something to eat and drink might be best.

Conner willingly volunteered to sit with Savi while Jade rehydrated and had a bite to eat. Rico sat down with Jade on a large flat rock about ten feet away from Conner and Savi.

"Rico, I just can't bear the thought of losing her. She's so young and the best friend I think I've ever had."

"Savi's a strong little thing. If she was going to die, I'm guessing it would have happened by now. She's still not out of the woods, though… " Rico paused a moment. "Did I just say that out loud?"

A half-smile crept across Jade's face as she punched Rico hard on his good arm.

"Quit joking around," she said in a scolding tone.

"Okay, calm down. It was just a slip of the tongue," he admitted. "You know how badly I want her to make it," he added sincerely.

"I know. I'm just so scared we're going to lose her," Jade confessed.

Conner sat next to Savi holding her hand. Suddenly, she squeezed it tight and yelled out, "Killed my brother! And…just…five years old!" Then she released Conner's hand and slipped back into unconsciousness.

Jade and Rico heard Savi yelling and ran over to see what had happened.

"What's going on?" Jade asked. She flashed an anxious look in Conner's direction.

"She's delirious. She yelled something about her brother being killed."

Jade pressed Conner, "Do you think that really happened?"

"Who knows, but I wouldn't put too much stock in anything she says in this condition. Her system is fighting the venom. There's a lot going on in that little body of hers right now."

The clouds had threatened rain all day, but it never really materialized until the moment Conner spoke his last word. All at once, a heavy downpour started. Within seconds, everything and everyone was soaking wet. Though they tried their best to protect Savi, she was soon sopping wet and lying in a large puddle of water, adding to an already difficult situation.

"We've got to move her," Rico suggested. "Let's get her over onto that flat rock. If we don't, she going to get pneumonia on top of everything else she's fighting."

"Should we risk moving her?" Jade asked.

"No choice," Conner replied.

Carefully, the three of them lifted Savi and carried her about ten feet and laid her down on top of the flat rock. They did their best to dry her off and covered her with the small piece of tarp that once held the berries.

The rain continued for a couple of hours into the night before it finally stopped. Soon the dark clouds were gone, revealing a star-filled sky. Thankfully, not only had the rain moved on, but also the chilly air that had accompanied it. To the delight of the group, the night air was now cool instead of being achingly cold.

Rico and Conner cautiously worked their way down the goat trail again to gather twigs and wood to make a fire. They determined to build one as close to Savi as possible, without the flames endangering her. They hoped the warmth of the fire would speed up the drying of her clothes and keep her comfortable at the same time.

While they were down the hill gathering material for the fire, Jade tended to Savi. Suddenly, Savi started convulsing uncontrollably. This time she shook violently for several seconds before her body collapsed again.

At this point, Jade feared the worst and immediately bent down and placed her ear over Savi's mouth to see if she was still breathing. To her relief, she was, but just barely. Worried beyond measure, she leaned back with a sigh and again started tearing up about her friend's dire condition.

All of a sudden, Savi opened her eyes and whispered softly, "Jade, can I have some water?" Her face was ashen, like she'd seen a ghost, but she was alive and that's all that mattered. Shocked but elated, Jade searched about the camp area to find a water bottle and quickly brought it back. Carefully, she propped up Savi's head and held the bottle for her as she drank down about a quarter of its contents.

"Oh my God, Savi, we thought you were going to die. You've been in and out of consciousness for almost a day. How are you feeling?"

"Like I got bit by a rattlesnake. Leg…killing," Savi whispered incoherently as she closed her eyes and fell back asleep.

Rico and Conner finally made it back up the slippery goat trail to the hilltop. Jade saw them coming toward her, each carrying a load of wood. Immediately she shouted out, "Savi woke up and she talked to me!"

Dropping the wood, Rico and Conner ran over to Jade and checked on Savi themselves.

"Okay now, what happened?" Rico inquired.

"Savi woke up and asked me to get her some water. I couldn't believe it. She knows a rattlesnake bit her and everything. I really thought we'd lost her for a minute, and then she just came to."

"Maybe somebody is watching over her," Rico said, "because, honestly, I thought she was a goner. Listen ... it's been a crazy day. You guys stay close to the fire and get some sleep. I'll stand guard a few hours and keep an eye on Savi. Conner, will you help me bring some of that wood closer to the fire? I'd like to keep it going as long as we can."

"How do you think Savi will feel tomorrow? Do you think she'll be well enough to travel?" Jade asked.

Rico paused a moment, then answered the question. "I sure hope so. Savi's health has to be our number one priority, but the truth is, we now only have four days left to get across the Susquehanna before the dam opens."

CHAPTER TWENTY

During the night, Savi woke up several times. On one of those occasions she asked for a drink of water and something to eat. After she finished, she immediately fell back to sleep. She was no longer shaking or talking deliriously, and she now seemed mostly concerned about the painful wound on her calf. Conner had put a 'butterfly bandage' on it to pinch it shut. And though it was no longer bleeding, the discomfort from it was written all over Savi's face.

By morning, Savi was sitting up, still woozy but talking like her old self. After they told her about all the craziness she had missed while she was unconscious, they ate breakfast together. Unfortunately, because of their extended stay on the hilltop due to Savi's injury, the provisions Luke had given them were almost gone.

Though she was feeling much better, Savi was still too weak to hike through the woods. They all knew the time they had to cross the Susquehanna River was ticking away, and that they weren't leaving anytime soon. Rico and Conner also realized that they had to come up with a new plan if there was any hope of crossing the river in time.

As the teens huddled around Savi, Rico and Conner told the girls about their idea to help the group start moving north again toward Camp Arrowhead. Rico had modified his backpack to serve as a carrier for Savi. He suggested that he and Conner alternate carrying her through the woods, that is, until she could walk on her own. Savi vehemently objected. She immediately got up and tried to show everyone that she could walk on her own, only to fall down writhing in pain after just a few steps.

Conner helped her up, and then proceeded to scold her; "Savi, for such a smart girl, that was a stupid thing to do."

Rico interrupted him. "Now listen, we've got to move. We're out of water, low on food, and running out of time. If we hope to cross the river before the deadline, we have to get moving!"

"You'll probably be able to walk better tomorrow, but today you can't," Conner added emphatically.

"Savi, I think it's a good idea" Jade interjected. "At least it will get us moving again, and let's face it, you're in no condition to walk right now."

Savi bowed her head and thought for a long time about what they said. Resignation settled into her features. "Alright, if you guys agree that as soon as I can walk, I'm out of the papoose. Deal?"

"Deal," everyone agreed.

Savi was soon tied in place and rode on the crude litter made out of Rico's modified backpack. Obviously, this mode of transport was extremely uncomfortable for her but despite the pain in her calf she refused to complain. In fact, she was extremely touched by the love and care the others showed her.

The group carefully eased their way down the still slippery goat trail, thinking how grateful they were for the hilltop that had been their home and refuge the past couple of days.

Once they entered the woods again, Rico was careful to ensure that Savi's wounded calf stayed clear of the underbrush. It was now late morning and the beating sun made carrying her that much more difficult. After about a half an hour, they came upon a small stream where they drank freely and rested. Before they left, they filled their water bottles and canteens. Conner had already told Rico he'd carry Savi for a while.

"Hey Savi, how's the ride back there?" he quizzed her.

"The truth is, it sucks," Savi shot back wearily. "Nice horse, lousy saddle."

"You must be getting better. You're a little pistol again," Conner joked between breaths. "I hope you tip well."

"Here's your tip," Savi said in a sincere tone. "I really appreciate what you're doing for me."

"Was that a compliment? Next you'll tell me you like me or something."

"Whoa, horsey," Savi countered. "I wouldn't go that far."

"You're killing me up here," Conner howled. "I need a break before I drop you."

Realizing he had carried her for about a half an hour, he gently helped her down and collapsed to the ground. Once stopped, everyone drank and rested.

Then the routine continued all over again. Rico and Conner were gratified to see Jade feeling strong. Since the rafting accident she had recovered slowly, but now, she carried a spear and did a good job keeping up with the pace. Though she was understandably tired like everyone else, she looked healthier than she had in days.

The boys took turns carrying Savi, until they could hardly walk. By early evening, they discovered that they were still a mile away from the spot Luke had marked out on the map for them to stop for the night. Completely spent, Rico and Conner conceded they'd have to bunk down for the night in the open woods, exposed.

After an extended time of rest, the group began setting up camp. In order to fortify their position, they stacked branches about four-feet high in a circular area eight-feet wide. They fashioned a narrow opening that served as a passageway in and out of the camp. It was behind this makeshift fortress that they chose to spend the night.

Night had fallen. And though there was plenty of water to drink, they had depleted their supply of dried fruit, and were down to their last three pieces of deer jerky. Jade knew that Savi hadn't eaten much since she was bitten. She also recognized that the boys were famished from carrying her friend all day. Touched by their acts of kindness, she responded in kind. She took out the last three pieces of jerky and handed one to each of them. When they protested she made a joke, claiming that she wasn't hungry and that she needed to watch her figure.

"I thought that was my job," Conner crowed.

"You sound like you drank too much rattlesnake venom," Jade countered with a wry smile. "Eat your jerky and shut up."

Everyone was too hungry and tired to argue with her. So after they all said, "thanks," they happily wolfed down the last strips of jerky.

Then, in the distance, the teens heard wolves howling. Fortunately for them, they sounded like they were at least a mile away, if not further. Nonetheless, the howls instantly sent cold chills up the girls' spines, bringing back frightful memories of the waterfall incident.

Rico and Conner had mustered up the energy to gather some more wood and make a fire. All of them leaned in close around it warming themselves and talking about the day's events.

Suddenly, a branch snapped a short distance away, and then another. Something was close and getting closer. Conner grabbed his spear and the girls pulled out their knives. Rico reached for his pistol and was just about to stand up, when the group heard a familiar voice.

"Hey now, don't go shooting at me," Luke yelled out, half-kidding.

Then Luke suddenly appeared in front of the barricade of branches that surrounded them.

"You scared us to death, Luke. What are you doing here?"

"Can I sit with you guys a couple minutes?"

"Sure," they replied in unison.

Luke squeezed into the camp through the narrow passageway. After exchanging pleasantries with everyone, he sat down in front of the fire.

"Honestly, I expected you to be much further along on your journey," he began, concern tinting his voice.

"Savi was bitten by a rattlesnake yesterday morning and almost died," Rico said. "We couldn't move her until just before noon today. Conner and I took turns carrying her."

Luke looked Savi over. "Sounds like you've had a rough go of it," he said. "Where'd the rattler get you?"

"Here on my leg," she replied as she pointed to her bandage.

"How are you doing now?" Luke asked.

"I'm getting better all the time. I'm guessing I'll be able to walk some by tomorrow," she predicted.

"Well don't overdo it. It'll take a couple days for that venom to clear your system."

Luke paused a moment and studied her smudged face as it glowed in the firelight. Then he said, "You're lucky you made it, Savi. Many don't." Then he looked at the visible signs of injury each of them was sporting and shook his head. "I wish I knew a good doctor in the area because you all look like you could use one."

"I'd say," Jade agreed.

"Now, be careful to keep those wounds disinfected and as clean as you can," he cautioned.

Luke then changed the subject and asked them how their provisions were holding up. They hesitated to admit it at first, but finally confessed that they were all out of food. Hearing this, he reached in his pack and gave them what appeared to be half of his provisions.

"No, we can't," Jade protested. "It wouldn't be right."

"Not right is leaving you here to die of starvation." He flashed a smile at her. "I'll be alright. There's plenty of stuff to eat out here."

"Are you sure?" Rico asked.

"I insist—before I leave, I'll show you some berries, mushrooms, and even nuts out here you can eat."

"Thanks, Luke," Jade acknowledged. "I don't believe that any of us would still be alive if it weren't for you."

"I'm not sure that's true. But, I'd like to see you get back to Arrowhead safely," he said in earnest.

"It's great to see you again, Luke," Savi confessed.

"Glad you feel that way and the feeling's mutual. Unfortunately…I didn't come for a social visit," he said in an ominous voice. "I'm here to warn you."

"Warn us…about what?" everybody asked at the same time.

"Vexel. I've been tracking him. And I'm convinced he's close by."

CHAPTER TWENTY-ONE

The fire began to die down and the weary travelers started to nod off one by one. Luke was also tired but he knew that Vexel often hunted at night. Since he had picked up his trail earlier, he decided that he would continue tracking him the next couple of hours before packing it in for the night.

Luke had already said his good-byes, so he decided to leave hoping not to wake them. Unexpectedly, everyone was startled awake by the hideous sound of animals fighting in the distance. The yelping and crying sounds of a dying animal were horrible. It sounded like it could be the work of Vexel.

Immediately, Luke said another good-bye to everyone and rushed out of the camp and back into the darkened woods. Everyone was concerned about the horrific noises they had just heard in the distance, especially in light of Luke's warning about Vexel prowling the area.

Rico put some more wood on the fire and volunteered to take the first shift, but Savi overruled him. She knew Rico and Conner had worked extra hard carrying her through the woods and needed a good night's sleep. Rico was too tired to resist and fell asleep in no time, his trusted spear by his side.

Rico gave Savi the pistol before he went to sleep. She tucked it away safely in her front vest pocket. In addition to the pistol, she had Conner's spear leaning against the branch wall at arm's length near the passageway. If anything happened, she'd have it in her hands in a fraction of a second.

With the exception of wolves howling not far from where they hunkered down for the night, Savi's first couple of hours on watch were uneventful.

Jade and Savi had decided to take the first two shifts, and it was nearing the time to rouse Jade for her watch. After Savi had been on duty for three hours, she tossed a few branches on the fire, and then decided to wake Jade.

After she roused her awake, Savi gently pulled the pistol out of her vest pocket and proceeded to show Jade how to use it, just in case. Both girls hoped it wouldn't come to that, but they also thought it wise to be prepared. After talking softly for a couple minutes, Savi slid over and went to sleep.

Jade was almost three hours into her watch when Rico woke up. After taking a drink from his water bottle, he moved over and sat next to her.

"Sleep well?" Jade asked.

"Like a rock. I was wiped after yesterday," he admitted. "What about you? How long have you been up?"

"Just a couple hours. I slept okay. Those animals fighting—kind of freaked me out," Jade replied after she took a quick look around. "Do you think we're going to make it, Rico?"

"Are you talking about making it to the river on time or making it out of here alive?" Rico asked.

"Both," she said.

"Why wouldn't we make it? Luke's hunting Vexel, and we're only about eighteen miles from Arrowhead. We just have to keep making progress. But getting to the river on time will be tough," Rico acknowledged. "It all depends on how Savi's leg does and how quickly she recovers...Today's a big day. We've got to get started early and go at least five miles if there's any hope of crossing the river before the dam opens," he acknowledged.

Jade grabbed Rico's hand and turned to look at his weary but handsome face. "I should have asked you earlier, but I'm hoping you don't have a girlfriend. Do you?" she asked, fearful of the answer.

"I'm not going to lie to you Jade. I do," Rico admitted.

Jade dropped his hand and turned away. "Then why did you kiss me the other night?" she asked in a hushed but angry tone.

"Because you're the girlfriend I'm talking about," he admitted with a grin.

Turning back quickly and grabbing his hand again, she scolded him. "Rico, I can't believe you did that to me." Then her face changed and she said adoringly, "Really, I'm your girlfriend?"

"Yeah. Is that okay? That is unless you're taken. I thought maybe you had the hots for Conner," he said in a kidding tone.

"Rico, stop it. You know better than that."

Like he had done the other night, Rico pulled Jade close and kissed her softly. She rested her head on his shoulder and the two sat in front of the fire for the next few minutes looking like two people in love.

Jade lifted her head and looked at Rico blissfully and thought to herself, *This is the happiest I've ever been in my whole life.*

Nearby, birds began to stir as the morning light increased minute by minute. The sound of the chirping of the crickets faded and was replaced by the birds singing wildly as they welcomed the new day.

Rico woke Savi and Conner and encouraged them to begin collecting their gear so they could get an early start on the day's hike. Following a quick breakfast of dried fruit and water, they prepared to leave the enclosure for the next camp about five miles to the north.

In the morning light, everyone saw that Savi moved on her feet much better than they had expected, particularly, since a rattlesnake bit her just two days earlier. Obviously, her improved mobility was a welcome relief to Jade, but even more so to Rico and Conner.

"How's it feeling, Savi?" Rico inquired.

"It's still sore, but I'm getting around much better today. I should be able to walk on my own, at least for a while," Savi contended.

"Well, give it a shot. But you've got to tell us if you get into trouble, promise?" Conner interjected.

After a pause, Savi agreed, "Come on, let's get started. We've got a long way to go."

Not long after they had left it, the enclosure they had built was out of sight behind trees, shrubs, and bushes. Conner and Rico had decided to set a slower pace in order not to overwhelm Savi. This enabled her to keep up as the group made slow but steady progress.

To their surprise and delight, the terrain suddenly changed. Now leaving the thick underbrush and dense forest, they found themselves in an open plain at least a half a mile wide and a mile or more long. At the beginning of the clearing was a small stream where they filled their empty canteens and water bottles.

Following a short break, they proceeded to cross the plain. After walking through the difficult underbrush and dense forest for the last few days, the open plain was a welcome change. Unhindered by obstacles, they were able to double their pace, Savi with them. By mid-morning, however, her limp worsened and the pace slowed once again.

The group now had to take rest breaks about every fifteen minutes in order to prevent having to carry Savi. While they relaxed near the end of the large plain they saw behind them a herd of elk crossing the open space. Without any warning, the herd broke into a run and headed straight for them. At first they weren't sure what was happening. But when a pack of wolves appeared behind them, it all made sense.

The elk zigzagged back and forth in an effort to shake the pursuing wolves. But the wolf pack was relentless. They mirrored the herd's every move with lightning-fast reactions. Turn for turn, cut for cut, they were right on their heels.

"We've got to make a run for the tree line!" Conner shouted.

"Savi can't run," Jade shouted back. "It's too far. She won't make it!"

"You're right…okay…you three get in a tight circle and face out. Savi, take my spear. I only have three bullets left. So I'll stand behind you guys in the middle with the pistol and try to shoot at least three of them. The rest we'll have to kill with our spears and knives."

The elk ran wild as they bore down on them. If they didn't turn, the group would be trampled to death by the stampeding herd. "Alright, here they come!" Rico yelled. "We've got to watch each other's backs."

All of a sudden, Jade panicked and started screaming. "We can't stay here. We're going to die!"

"Jade!" Savi yelled. "Pull it together."

"We're going to die!" Jade screamed more vehemently than before.

All at once, Savi, who was positioned next to Jade, slapped her hard across the face. The sound of skin hitting skin was so loud that the others heard it over the noise of the charging elk.

Jade, shocked by what her friend had just done, immediately stopped screaming. "Unless you pull it together, we are going to die!" Savi shouted at her in anger. "Now stop it, Jade!"

Jade quickly resumed her position, as did Savi. Looking up at the herd, the elk were now just fifty feet away and closing fast.

CHAPTER TWENTY-TWO

The charging elk, perceiving the group to be an obstacle or a threat, veered off to the right at the last minute. The herd of forty strong beasts blew past them, leaving them shocked and in a cloud of dust. Once they had passed by, the terrified onlookers waited for the wolves to appear out of the chalky haze in front of them, but they never did. Instead, to their amazement, they saw the vicious wolves over three hundred yards away. They had downed a straggler and were now in the process of devouring the helpless animal.

Although relieved, they knew the wolves would eventually finish eating the carcass and turn their attention elsewhere. So without delay, they made a beeline for the trees that were within a few hundred yards. Once hidden inside the tree line, they stopped to catch their breath and take a drink. But before they continued, the group looked back one final time. Despite the meal provided for them, the wolves snapped and snarled at one another over different parts of the fallen elk. This convinced them that they were no longer in imminent danger and lessened the stress they felt. Still, not wanting to take a chance, they moved in the opposite direction as fast and as far away from the wolves as possible.

Exhausted from the forced march, they finally stopped for a break. Savi made her way over to Jade who appeared to be not too happy to see her.

"Jade, I'm really sorry for slapping you the way I did—Will you forgive me?"

"You hit me really hard, Savi," Jade shot back in an angry tone. "Just like my mother does."

"I'm sorry, but it looked like you were losing it out there and I didn't know what else to do," she explained.

"I've been slapped in the face since I've been old enough to remember and I hate it more than anything," Jade fumed. "I never thought you'd do something like that to me."

"You deserve to be angry, Jade. Again, I'm really sorry. I've never slapped anyone in the face before. And I hope I never will again. I just wanted you to know how awful I feel."

"You should feel awful," Jade railed.

Unexpectedly, Rico spoke up. "Let's go you guys, we've got to keep moving. We lost a lot of time back there. Not to mention, the wolves could be finished eating and heading our way. Savi, you come up here and walk with me. Conner, you keep Jade in front of you and guard the rear."

"Sounds like my kind of job." Conner said with a grin.

"Shut up, Conner." Jade said rolling her eyes.

As they started moving north again, Rico could tell that Savi was struggling. Not only was she hurting physically, but she was devastated by Jade's apparent unwillingness to forgive her. Savi's limp was now more pronounced than before, and she was walking with her head down, obviously distressed about the situation with Jade.

While they were walking, Rico placed his hand on Savi's back and tried to encourage her. "For the record, you did the right thing out there, Savi. Don't get me wrong, I'm not advocating that you make a habit of slapping people, but in that situation, it was necessary."

"Thanks for saying that, Rico. But it doesn't change the fact that she is still really mad at me," Savi conceded. "I feel so bad that I slapped her at all, but the fact that I struck her so hard makes me feel even worse."

"Give her some time. She'll get over it," Rico assured her.

They had traveled about three miles since leaving their overnight camp and now were only two miles from the day's final stop.

"Hey Jade, how are you doing up there?" Conner inquired.

"Leave me alone," Jade replied harshly.

"Hey, don't bite my head off," he replied in an exasperated tone. "I was just checking to see how you're doing."

"Sorry, I'm just mad at Savi," she confessed.

"Why, because she smacked you?"

"Duh!" she shot back.

"Well, frankly…you needed it. We were in trouble and we needed you to help us. You were panicking. Something had to be done."

"Oh really," Jade fired back. "This coming from the guy hiding in the back of the raft after Doug fell out," she fumed. "No one is ever going to hit me in the face again without getting whacked back."

"Sounds like you get slapped a lot, huh?" Conner questioned.

"Shut up," she blurted in a huff. "I'm done talking to you."

"Fine. Whatever …."

It was now late afternoon and they had been walking since early morning. Savi was hurting and completely spent, and there was still about a quarter mile to go before they reached the spot that Luke had marked on the map. Rico realized that the group could not make the last quarter mile without an extended break, so they took one.

During the rest stop everyone drank most of their remaining water and ate what was left of the diminished stock of food Luke had so kindly provided. Jade and Savi sat alone apart from each other, separated by about ten feet. The guys ate and drank together and then Rico went over and sat with Jade. At the same time, Conner went to sit with Savi.

"I heard you and Conner fighting while we were walking. What was going on?" Rico inquired.

"Nothing. Everything's fine."

"Okay, if that's how you want it," Rico nodded and started to leave.

"No, don't go. I'm sorry…I'm just so mad at Savi," Jade grumbled angrily. "And then Conner had to open his big mouth."

"What did he say that made you so mad?"

"He said he thought that Savi was right to slap me," she protested.

"She was," Rico confirmed.

"What! You think so too?"

"Yeah, I do. We needed you out there, and you were losing it. What do you think she should have done?" Rico asked.

Jade turned away from him after his question and railed, "I'm done with this conversation. I can't believe you're taking her side."

"I'm not taking anyone's side. I'm just telling you what you need to hear," Rico let out a sigh. When she didn't respond, he got up and walked away.

The tears welled up until Jade couldn't hold them in anymore. She began to cry. Savi started to get up to go talk with her, but Rico grabbed her arm.

"No Savi, I think she's got to work this one out on her own," Rico counseled. "I think it's better if we leave her alone for a while."

The needed break lasted about an hour. Jade sat alone for the remainder of the time. Once they were all rested, Rico instructed the group to gather up their things and prepare to walk the last quarter mile to the camp. Still weary, hurting, and now stiff from the extended break, everyone struggled to get up but finally they did.

This time Conner led the way, with Jade close behind him. Savi was next, and Rico brought up the rear. Rico hoped that he wouldn't have to carry Savi again. By the way she was limping, he thought he might have to.

Eventually, they arrived at their destination. It was early evening, though enough light remained so that they could see the place was perfect for them. There was a small stream surrounded by several large clusters of huckleberry bushes and a good supply of edible mushrooms. Across the stream stood a rock formation with a narrow but deep cave that would serve as their refuge. Relieved, they saw that the only access to the cave was through the limited opening that was three-feet wide and four-feet high. Even Savi had to duck in order not to bump her head on the entrance opening.

Although everyone was tired, they all had things they needed to do, such as set up and secure their new camp. As they had done the last couple of days, Rico and Conner gathered wood for a fire. They also carved sharp tips on branches they used to fortify the cave entrance against predators. Down by the stream, Savi picked enough huckleberries and mushrooms to last the group for a few days. Jade was assigned the task of filling everyone's canteen and water bottles.

Rico lit the fire and everyone gathered around it. Once settled, they ate the berries, mushrooms, and drank the replenished water supply till they were satisfied. Despite having met their physical needs, an air of tension still hung over the group, evidenced by an extended period of silence after the meal.

All of a sudden Jade spoke up. "I've thought a lot about what happened today. And I need to apologize for my behavior out on the field...and my bad attitude...when I saw the elk charging at us, and the pack of wolves behind them, I freaked out. Obviously, I didn't handle myself well. I started to panic and wanted to run. Savi, I know when you hit me it wasn't done to hurt me, but it did…you were trying to help me pull it together. I forgive you for hitting me and I'm sorry for letting all of you down out there." She reached over and took Savi's hand. "I know your apology earlier was sincere. But I just wasn't ready to hear or accept it. You guys need to know that my mother has slapped me in the face for as long as I can remember. And honestly, I hate her for it…when I was slapped today, it brought all that stuff up for me…I'm tired of being hit." Jade began to sob.

Rico and Savi immediately surrounded Jade with their arms.

"Jade, I'm so sorry," Savi whispered in her ear. "I had no idea what you've gone through before you got here."

"I know. You did what you had to today. I guess I needed it for once. God knows it worked," she said in a consoling voice.

"Jade, I'm proud of you," Rico said in an affirming tone. "I know what you said couldn't have been easy, especially with what you just told us."

"Have you ever told anybody about this before?" Savi asked choking back her own tears.

"I told my aunt, but she told me that if it got out, it would bring shame on our family," Jade confided. "So I've just kept it to myself."

"Jade, abuse is wrong. I've been swatted on occasion when I was young for being disrespectful, but there's a big difference between that and being hit in the face continually."

"She's right. What she's doing to you is wrong. You have every right to report her.... You know, to the police."

Jade paused for a minute then said with conviction, "I promise, when I get home I'm going to make it clear that if she ever hits me again, I'll call the police."

Everyone sat quietly and pondered the issue at hand. Then Jade looked across the fire at Conner and added, "I'm sorry to you also. I know you were just telling me what I needed to hear today, and I snapped at you. I hope you can forgive me."

A broad grin broke across Conner's face. "Only if you let me have your share of the berries tomorrow. I'm not getting enough to eat around here."

Jade hadn't smiled all day until then. In fact, everyone was now laughing. Even Rico thought Conner's quip was funny. It seemed like it had been a long time since they'd all had a good laugh together. Unfortunately, they wouldn't be laughing for long.

CHAPTER TWENTY-THREE

The fire dwindled down to hot embers and Conner extinguished it with water from the stream. Savi then grabbed the medical kit and disinfected Rico's and Conner's wounds. Rico's injury was healing with no sign of infection. However, Conner's facial cut was deep and still inflamed. Savi decided to use the remaining peroxide to thoroughly disinfect the gash so that it wouldn't get any worse. After gently sterilizing the wound she put a fresh bandage on it to keep it dry and clean.

Once inside the cave, the group discussed their ideas about guard duty. Everyone admitted that they were physically and emotionally drained from the events of the day. No one felt confident they could stay awake for a two-hour shift, so they decided to reduce the watch times to just one hour. Though very tired, Rico reluctantly volunteered to take the first shift.

Following the discussion the tired girls disappeared into the cave. They laid down on makeshift pine needle mattresses they had put together shortly after arriving at the new camp. In minutes, they were fast asleep.

The guys fortified the entrance as usual with strategically placed stakes designed to keep predators from penetrating their refuge. Once they finished, Conner elected to stay up a few minutes to chat with Rico. Taking out a water bottle he had filled earlier, Conner leaned over and offered Rico a drink. He took the bottle gladly and sucked down several greedy gulps.

"I think you're doing a great job out here, Rico," Conner said sincerely. "You and Savi have proven yourselves to be strong leaders in some really tough situations."

"Thanks, Conner, that's nice of you to say. So now that we're tossing compliments around, I've been thinking…you're not half the jerk I thought you were when I first met you," Rico acknowledged.

Conner stared at him with a puzzled look. "Was that supposed to be a compliment?"

Rico flashed a quick smile. "That's how I meant it."

Conner looked into the cave at the girls sleeping. "Wow, can you believe Savi? She is really something isn't she?"

Rico glanced over at her. "Yeah, I'd say so."

"I've never met anyone like her before. She's a really caring person, but tough as nails at the same time," Conner noted.

"I wonder if that's how they raise 'em in Mississippi, a Bible in one hand and a pistol in the other," Rico replied jokingly.

"And how about Jade? She's pretty special too. You're lucky she's all into you…I thought I had a chance at first, but now…it's clear you're the man," Conner conceded.

"I'm glad you figured that out. Saves me from having to tie you to a tree and leave you behind for Vexel," Rico said kiddingly.

Shaking his head, Conner looked over at Rico smiling. "That's a nice thought to sleep on. I'd better go lay down before you get the rope out…See you in the morning, Rico." Conner quietly slipped into the cave.

"Goodnight, *hot dog*," Rico shot back with a grin.

Rico stood alone at the entrance. The smell of pine mixed with the lingering smoke from the fire scented the air. In minutes, everyone but Rico was sound asleep. He had worked hard all day and late into the night, and it had finally caught up with him. After only twenty minutes on watch he started to nod off. Instead of standing up and walking around, he foolishly decided to sit down behind the stakes by the entrance. In no time, he drifted off to sleep himself.

Outside the cave a cunning group of predators lurked nearby. A new pack of wolves had detected a tempting scent and followed it to the cave. Crouching low, they silently inched their way closer with every careful step.

Inside, Rico slept like a baby, oblivious of the deadly threat outside. The lead wolf placed his front paw gently on a rock by the cave's opening. He used the strength of his hind legs and quietly lifted himself up. His head was now high enough to see what he had only smelled up until this point. His steely eyes darted back and forth and then fixed on Rico sleeping behind the wooden stakes just a few feet away. The others crowded forward behind the lead wolf sensing a killing moment.

Suddenly, one of the predators lurched forward and tussled with another wolf hoping to get a better look at their unsuspecting victim. The aggravated wolf spun around and bit the pest, which yelped in protest.

Startled awake, Rico reached for the pistol just as the lead wolf leaped in the air toward him.

"Conner!" Rico shouted.

Conner sprang to his feet and grabbed his spear. Both Savi and Jade awoke and screamed simultaneously. The lead wolf also let out a horrible cry when it failed to clear the stakes and was impaled in the stomach. Wails of pain filled the air as it struggled to free itself less than two feet from Rico. Feeling sorry for the animal that tried to kill him moments before, he lifted the pistol and shot the wolf once, until it lay dead. The rest of the wolves beat a hasty retreat.

Blood flowed freely onto the cave floor from the dead wolf's multiple wounds. Traumatized, the group took a moment and caught their breath, then turned angrily to Rico.

Savi looked at him in disbelief. "How did the wolves get so close to the cave without you alerting us?"

Rico paused a long time before answering. So long, that Savi felt she needed to repeat the question.

"Rico…I asked you…how did the wolves get so close without you waking us?"

Faced with Savi's pointed questions, Rico was tempted to lie. But, he didn't. Instead, he reluctantly told them the shameful truth.

"I fell asleep."

"You what? You fell asleep?" everyone protested at the same time.

"That's what I said," Rico snapped back. "I fell asleep."

"Really! That's something I'd expect from Conner, not from you," Savi scolded.

Conner shot her an agitated look. "Gee thanks, Savi. Glad to know you've got so much confidence in me."

"Sorry, Conner," Savi continued as she stared at Rico, "but I can't believe you put all our lives in jeopardy instead of waking up one of us."

Suddenly, growls sounded from outside near the entrance. This time everyone was prepared and had their weapon in hand. Carefully, they looked out and realized the relentless pack of wolves had gathered again, moving slowly but steadily toward the enclosure.

Rico whispered to the others, "I've only got two shots left in the pistol, and I see four of them."

"Savi, you said you could shoot a pistol, right?" Rico asked.

"Yeah, I can shoot," she replied.

"Okay, here's the pistol. I'll use the spear." Rico handed her the gun. "There are two bullets left. You've got to kill two of them, Savi. Take good aim and don't miss," he added firmly.

Conner and Rico planted themselves behind the dead wolf impaled on a stake and pointed their spears toward the other approaching wolves. Savi stood between them with her pistol raised and looked for a good shot. Jade hid behind the others with knife in hand, her body shaking with fear.

Savi leaned forward and whispered, "I've got a clear shot at the one closest on the right."

"When you're ready, take it," Rico whispered back.

Moments later a shot fired and the targeted wolf fell to the dirt. The other wolves again dashed back into the woods.

"Nice shot, Savi, you got 'em!" Conner exclaimed triumphantly.

"One down," Rico added.

"Here they come again," Conner warned.

Again the unyielding pack started to advance on the enclosure. This time the three remaining animals moved boldly forward, growling with every step, almost as if they realized that the element of surprise was now gone. Just as she had done before, Savi trained her pistol on the lead wolf. He growled viciously and steadily pressed closer. She took aim and waited for the right moment, then fired the last bullet. Instantly, the wolf hit the ground. It quivered momentarily and then fell perfectly still. The remaining two wolves appeared to have had enough and disappeared across the creek and into the woods.

"Savi, that was awesome," Jade said from behind.

Rico grabbed Savi's shoulder, spun her around and hugged her. "You weren't kidding when you said you can shoot."

"All that target practice on the farm just paid off," Savi said with a sigh.

After taking a minute to calm down, they used Savi's small flashlight to survey their surroundings. It was a bloody mess. One wolf was dead on the stakes just inside the cave entrance, while two other animals lay still and bleeding a few feet apart just outside the enclosure.

Suddenly, in the distance about a mile away, they heard two distinct rifle shots.

Savi immediately perked up and turned to the others. "Listen…We've got to get out of here, now! I'll bet that was Luke firing at what he thinks is Vexel. Remember when he told us Vexel loves the smell of blood. Look around. There's blood everywhere." The others quickly agreed and, in a matter of minutes, they gathered their gear and left the cave. Both Savi and Conner accidentally got blood on themselves climbing over the dead wolf at the entrance, so they used the stream water to clean themselves off before leaving the area. Savi hurriedly knelt down and used her map and compass to figure out the best route to the next camp. They departed right away for the new location and headed in the direction Savi determined to be the quickest.

Savi feared that Vexel was closer to them than ever before. Then her thoughts shifted to Luke. She hoped the rifle shots they heard had killed Vexel and prayed they weren't Luke's final shots before the beast killed him.

Moving through the dark wilderness, Savi wondered for the first time if her dad would ever walk her down the aisle the way she'd always dreamed, or if he'd be attending her funeral instead. Her head began swirling with thoughts of home and how much she missed everyone she'd left behind. Then, unexpectedly, a low hanging branch that Jade had brushed past snapped back and slapped Savi in the face, instantly bringing her back into the moment.

"Ow!" Savi, blurted out.

"What happened?" Jade asked, turning around.

"A branch smacked me in the face," Savi grumbled.

Concerned, Jade stopped. "Are you okay? Do you want to stop a minute?"

"No, we've got to keep moving," Savi, insisted. "I'll be fine."

Before the four had taken their next step, they heard the gruesome roars of what sounded like a big, angry animal behind them about a mile off. Its deep growl scared them down to the bone. No one said a word. They just kept sledging through the woods as swiftly as the conditions allowed. But they all had the same nagging question swirling through their heads.

Could that be Vexel?

CHAPTER TWENTY-FOUR

Walking through the dense forest at night was tough enough. Trying to do it quietly was nearly impossible, especially with the moonlight barely penetrating the thick canopy. Once again Savi used her small flashlight, map, and compass to determine the shortest possible route to their next camp spot.

By one o'clock in the morning the group had traveled a couple of miles from the cave. Exhausted from lack of sleep and the difficult night's trek, they stopped for an extended rest. They discussed the possibility of setting up camp at their current location, but recalling those awful sounds they heard earlier, they decided to keep moving.

While studying the map, Savi noticed an alternative campsite that Luke had pointed out. She remembered he told her it was another safe haven if they felt strong enough to continue past the cave they had just left. She discovered that it was only about a half mile farther from their current location. With a renewed sense of purpose, the weary travelers agreed to make the alternative refuge their new destination. Fortunately, a short time later the forest thinned out, which increased the moonlight and improved visibility. This made moving through the woods faster and somewhat easier.

Before long, they arrived at the place where Luke assured them there was a sheltered campsite. Not seeing it right away, they spread out to search for it. After scouring the area for several minutes, Conner eventually found what they were looking for, halfway up a hill near a group of rocks and behind some pine trees. The cave was hidden so well that without the map, they would have never found it.

Savi and Jade used the remainder of their strength to gather up pine needles. Like before, they used them to cover the floor of the cave to lessen the chill from the cold ground. At the same time, Rico and Conner collected and sharpened stakes to fortify the entrance to the enclosure in the usual way. After a brief discussion, the group opted not to build a fire for fear they might give away the location of their hiding place.

The entrance was situated so that the moon shined directly into the first few feet of it. The weary quartet sat down together surrounded by moonlight and ate yesterday's berries and drank their fill. Savi again checked Conner's facial wound and noticed a marked improvement from the day before. Once she finished with Conner everyone sat quietly until Jade spoke up.

"I hope Luke's alright," she said, starting to recover from the tough hike. "He must have been shooting at Vexel when we heard those shots earlier today."

"Well, judging by the horrible sounds after that, he must have missed him," Conner lamented.

"Hopefully, those three dead wolves gave Vexel plenty to eat for the time being," Savi interjected.

Rico had been unusually quiet since the wolf incident and seemed deeply troubled. Savi broke the ice and asked the question on everyone's mind.

"Rico, what's the matter?"

He sat silent and lowered his chin. Then quiet tears fell onto his hands folded on his lap. Though the others were dog-tired, they slid over and surrounded him.

"What's going on?" Jade whispered softly.

Rico lifted his dust-covered brow and exposed the fresh tear tracks on his sullen face. He didn't answer Jade's question at first. But after a moment's thought, he finally did. "I…almost got us killed," he confessed. "I really messed up by falling asleep on my shift."

After reaffirming his blunder, he lowered his head again in shame. Savi let him sit quietly a minute before she reached over, lifted his chin, and turned his face toward hers. She looked him in the eyes and did her best to encourage him. "Yeah, Rico, you did fall asleep and that wasn't good. But it's been hell out here. And you've been a great leader and super responsible the whole time up until you fell asleep on your watch. We're all wiped out, and it could have happened to any one of us." She paused a moment, as if another thought slipped into her head. "And one more thing, I was too hard on you back at the cave and I apologize for that."

"Savi's right, Rico. You've been an awesome leader and have done your best to protect us ever since we lost Doug," Jade said, doing her best to reassure him also.

"It's true, Rico. It could have been any one of us. Glad it was you and not me...but it could have been any one of us," Conner added clumsily.

"Nice, Conner, that was helpful," Savi fired back.

Rico shook his head and fought back a smile. Then he took a minute and studied his new friends faces. "I feel so stupid. I don't think I've cried in front of anyone since my mom died."

"Sometimes we all need a good cry," Savi offered. "I've heard it said, 'it cleanses the soul.'"

Rico pondered her words.

"You're probably right, Savi. I've been through a tough time since my mom died. My dad still hasn't recovered and he's gone a lot. I've been trying my best to take care of my brothers and sister...There's just a lot on my plate right now." Then he continued, "I feel like you guys are already more than just friends...and I've known you less than a week. You know more about me than most people I've known for years. Thanks for forgiving my screw-up. It won't happen again," he promised.

"We know it won't," Savi said to encourage him.

Again, Rico looked slowly at the others one by one and said, "I wouldn't want to be out here with anybody else but you guys...Well maybe except for you, Conner," he said kiddingly with a smirk on his face.

"Gee, thanks for the love," Conner countered, shaking his head in amusement.

Rico smiled in Conner's direction and thanked everyone for their support. Then he lay down near the entrance. Putting his hands behind his head, he appeared to be deep in thought as he looked up at the brilliant three-quarter moon. Once he was settled down, Jade went and sat down next to him. After several minutes, she gently placed her head on his chest. No words were exchanged nor did there need to be. Rico, comforted by her show of affection, put his arm around Jade and the two fell asleep next to each other.

Conner chose to take the first shift and quietly shooed Savi off, so she could get some rest. She went into the enclosure and used some pine needles to make a small bed. Before lying on it, Conner watched as Savi knelt down and spent some time praying. When she finished, she rolled on to her pine mattress and fell fast asleep.

Conner decided to extend his watch by an hour so that the others could get some extra rest. Eventually, he started to fade and decided it was time to wake Savi.

She took a few minutes to gather herself and then assumed the nightshift. It was now three-thirty in the morning and all was fairly quiet. Besides crickets chirping, and the occasional croaking of frogs, the night passed peacefully. Savi also lengthened her shift by half an hour before waking Jade. When she did, Rico stirred and woke up as well.

"Go back to sleep, Rico," Savi whispered. "It's Jade's turn."

"No, let her sleep. I'm awake now," he insisted.

Jade didn't argue at all and fell back to sleep almost immediately. Before Rico took over guard duty from Savi, he glanced over at her. There she stood by the entrance holding Conner's spear with a toughness and determination that brought a smile to his face. He rose to his feet, walked over to her and put his arm around her shoulder.

"You were right to come down hard on me after I fell asleep on my watch," he said to her sincerely. "There's no excuse for that. I put everyone in danger."

"Yeah, that's true. But we've already talked about that and nobody's perfect. We all make mistakes."

"True, but if somebody else did that...I'd have a hard time letting it go," he admitted. "You seem to be able to get over stuff quickly...I wish I could do that."

Then Savi moved out from under his arm and turned away. "I've had a lot of practice at forgiving, Rico. Way more than I'd like."

He glanced at her with a puzzled look on his face. "What does that mean, Savi?"

"It doesn't mean anything," she said, and then started to walk away. "I'm going back to sleep."

"Savi, come on, tell me what you're talking about?" Rico pressed her.

"It's too complicated and I'm too tired," she countered with tears welling up in her eyes. "How about I tell you another time."

"Promise?"

"Promise," she agreed. "Good night, Rico."

"Night, Savi."

By the end of Rico's shift, the dawn shimmered golden sunbeams through the woods and into the enclosure. The warmth of the sun brought welcome relief from what had been a chilly night.

Rico woke up Savi. Once she had rubbed the sleep out of her eyes, he asked her to grab the map and sit down with him. The map indicated they were about eleven miles from the Susquehanna River. Regrettably, they realized they still had to cross over a mountain range to get to the river and ultimately, Camp Arrowhead. Luke had predicted this would slow them down. Savi glanced over at Rico with a concerned look on her face and told him what he already knew.

"Today is August 29. We only have three days left to get across the river."

CHAPTER TWENTY-FIVE

Feeling a renewed sense of strength and urgency, Savi and Rico woke up Jade and Conner right away. They encouraged them to pack up quickly and prepare for the day's journey. Savi estimated they were about nine miles from the base of the mountain range they'd have to cross to get to the Susquehanna River. On the map Luke had marked out a sheltered camp at the foot of the mountains where they were planning to stay the night.

The nine-mile hike was the longest they had attempted to date. Fortunately, everyone felt rested and hopeful that the day's trek would get them within a day of the river, and that much closer to safety. The group determined to head out earlier than normal because they knew how many miles they had to travel to get to the next campsite.

Just after leaving the camp, everyone heard the thumping of a helicopter. Although their hopes were heightened for a moment, in the end, they were dashed once again. The copter never came close and appeared to fly down the river, which now was well over a mile to the east of them.

The morning weather was ideal when they left camp. In addition, within the first hour, the terrain changed significantly in their favor, allowing them to make swift progress. The thick underbrush was gone and the dense forest thinned out. By mid morning, they had already covered over three miles, leaving them six to go to reach the base of the mountains.

"Savi, keep your eyes open for anything to eat," Rico said after his stomach rumbled. "We ate the last of the berries and mushrooms this morning and I'm starving."

"I've looked for food since we left this morning but haven't seen a thing," Savi replied. "There's a lake on the map where we can catch some fish, but it's too far out of the way. I'm sick of berries, even though I'd eat some in a heartbeat right about now."

"Oh look, a Taco Bell!" Conner shouted from the rear.

"Shut up, Conner," Jade scolded him. "That's not even funny right now."

"Okay, Jade, now you're not getting any of my 'Burrito Supreme,'" he joked.

Suddenly, a clap of thunder in the distance interrupted their levity.

"Great, just what we need, a storm," Jade whined.

"The guys are starting to smell again. A little rain might not be all that bad," Savi said to Jade in a joking tone.

"Savi, behave," Jade said with a grin.

"I heard that," Rico hollered from behind.

"Me too," Conner added.

"Good, so take the hint," Savi said playfully.

Fearing another severe weather system was headed their way, the group pressed on even harder toward the new campsite. It was now mid-afternoon, and according to the map they were just two miles from their destination. The forced march was beginning to take its toll on them, and the weather was changing, minute-by-minute, from bad to worse. They were now walking in a thick mist that reminded Jade of a foggy summer morning in San Francisco.

In addition to the fog there were occasional downpours. When the rain was heavy the fog diminished. But once it stopped the heavy mist returned thicker than ever.

"Savi, try to keep the map dry," Rico yelled. "You better lead the way because I can't see ten feet in front of me and have no idea where we're going," he added.

"Okay, let's stop a minute so I can double-check our current position," Savi asked.

"Seriously, no one has anything to eat?" Conner said in a desperate tone. "I'm dying here."

"Want a bite of my 'Burrito Supreme,' Conner?" Jade quipped.

"Don't be obnoxious, Jade," he fired back.

"Hey, 'blankie boy,' not so funny now is it?" Jade replied.

"Really! Can you two stop a minute?" Savi barked. "I'm trying to figure out where we are."

"Okay," Conner said. "You don't have to bite our heads off."

"Alright, I think we're here…and we need to go that way." She pointed northwest.

"Are you sure?" Rico asked.

"As sure as I *can* be," she replied.

"Okay, Savi, you lead the way," Rico commanded. "Conner, you follow Savi, and, Jade, you go behind Conner. I'll bring up the rear."

By this time, the rain had stopped. In its absence, the mist had grown so thick they feared they'd lose sight of each other if they weren't careful. After walking another half an hour, everyone's confidence in Savi started to waver.

"Savi, it feels like we're going in circles," Conner said, concern tinting his voice. "Are you sure you know what you're doing?"

"I'm doing the best I can. I've never navigated in these kinds of conditions before. Here's the compass. Do you want to try?" she retorted angrily.

"Savi, we're all wiped out and we just don't want to walk further than we have to or go in the wrong direction," Rico said abruptly.

"I get it!" Savi responded. "I need you guys to chill out; if you can't trust me at least trust the compass. I'll have you know that I didn't sign up for this. Now, quit whining and follow me." She stormed off ahead of the others.

"You guys — stop it!" Jade snapped. "Leave her alone. She's trying her best. Can't you see she's already got enough pressure on her without you two questioning her every move?"

Savi stopped dead in her tracks and looked back. When they caught up with her again she kept the group pressing forward through the dense mist despite the protests of Rico and Conner. Unconcerned by their lack of confidence, Savi remained focused, periodically checking her map and compass. After trudging through the muddy ground for another hour, everyone felt exhausted, soaked, and hungry. Everyone's temper was now at the boiling point. Even Jade started to question Savi's navigational skills.

"Savi, are you sure we're not just going in circles?" she asked.

"Yeah Savi, this is ridiculous. You don't have any idea where we are or where we're going, do you?" Conner blurted out behind Jade.

"We just can't keep going like this much longer," Rico chimed in angrily.

Now limping noticeably with a strained look on her face, Savi turned back and shouted, "All I know is that the compass says we're moving northwest and I believe it. That means we're about a half an hour from the camp. If we stop now we're in real trouble. We've got to keep moving. Now, all of you need to suck it up and quit whining," she chided them emphatically. "If we don't find the camp in forty-five minutes, I'll give up myself," she said with sense of resignation.

Somehow, the group mustered the courage to continue slogging through the woods and mist in spite of their uncertainty about Savi's leadership. Then from in front of her, Jade heard Savi plead, "Lord, help me… show me the way…we've got to find this camp soon."

By now another half hour had passed and the protests multiplied.

"Savi, enough!" Rico yelled from the rear. "We need to stop now!"

"No, we've got to be close. Five more minutes is all I ask," she pleaded.

"No way, Savi, it's over!" Conner yelled.

"They're right, Savi, I can't go on anymore," Jade added. "We have to stop now. I'm done." She collapsed in a heap onto the muddy ground.

Savi let out a big sigh. "So, it's come to this? We're just going to lie down here and die? Well not me. The map says we're right on top of the camp and I'm going to find it."

"You just can't go off by yourself," Jade warned. "You'll get lost out there. We won't be able to see you after twenty feet in this mist."

"I'm not giving up, not yet anyway," Savi shot back.

"You're staying with us, Savi. That's it!" Rico yelled for emphasis.

"You're not my mother!" Savi screamed back. "I know we're close…and I'm going to look around."

Savi hobbled off and spent the next fifteen minutes searching in the mist for the elusive campsite without success. Weary and discouraged she started limping painfully back to the spot where the others had stopped. When she got close to where she thought they were, she yelled out for them. When they heard her shouts, the others yelled back. Savi followed their voices until she reached the spot where she had left them.

Though the mist was still thick and the rain had stopped, no one had the energy to talk, least of all Savi. Once again she pulled out the map and tried to figure out where the camp was. As soon as Rico, Jade, and Conner saw her with the map in her hands they began taunting her.

"What now, Savi?" Conner said mockingly. "Are you going to tell us we have another half an hour to go?"

"It's over, Savi, put the map away," Rico grumbled.

"You tried but we're lost…Just let it go…It's over," Jade said in a tone of resignation.

"I'm going to look for some food," Conner moaned. "I'll eat anything at this point."

"I'll go with you," Rico offered.

Savi sat hungry and exhausted, wondering what she had done wrong. She used the compass to guide her path and the map to check her bearings. She couldn't understand why she had missed the camp. Frustrated beyond measure, she bowed her head and began to sob. Jade was so tired from the walk that she didn't even have the strength to move over to console her. So there she sat alone crying in the thick mist wondering why her compass, map, and prayers had failed her.

Suddenly, Rico yelled out, "Where are you guys?"

"Here we are!" Jade shouted in response.

Moments later, Rico and Conner appeared out of mist with strange looks on their faces. They rejoined the girls and told them to follow them.

"Did you find some food?" Jade asked anxiously.

Rico and Conner didn't reply. Rico lifted Jade to her feet and Conner reached down and pulled Savi up as well.

"What are you doing?" she protested.

"Just come with us. You've got to see this," Conner insisted.

The two of them led the girls through the forest for several minutes, when all of a sudden some big rocks became visible. Then Conner grabbed Savi's hand, pulled her forward and pointed.

"Look Savi, it's the cave we've been trying to find. You did it Savi…You led us here."

Instantly, Savi started to cry again. She didn't say a word but instead dropped to her knees, bowed her head and whispered audibly, "Thank you."

Rico, Jade, and Conner watched as the faithful little warrior knelt before them and wept in gratitude. The three appeared embarrassed as they thought about how shamefully they had treated their courageous companion. Soon thereafter, the mist lifted and revealed a cloudless sky. Now, for the first time since midmorning, they could actually see their surroundings.

Amazingly, they were in a beautiful and enchanting area. A few hundred feet away a pond the size and shape of an ice rink was now visible. The pine forest sparkled in the late afternoon sunlight and the birds started singing for the first time since morning. The brilliant sun ignited the moisture on countless pine needles and they glistened beautifully. The view around them was nothing short of majestic.

The elusive cave was just a few feet above a small rock formation. It was about fifteen feet deep and the best part was that it was dry. The only thing lacking now was food.

Savi and Rico tried to fish the pond for a while, but they didn't even get a nibble. They were tempted to give up, but Savi looked inside Rico's small tackle box one more time. She found a little green cricket made out of soft plastic with a tiny hook sticking out of it. It took just a few seconds to tie the lure on the line and then cast it out a few feet. Letting it float on the surface of the pond she waited, and in a matter of minutes, there were swirls in the water near the lure. Then a fish took the cricket under. Savi set the hook by yanking back on the line and caught the first fish of the day. It was only about six inches long, but at least it was something.

Rico immediately took the fish and cleaned it. Then he went into the cave and gathered some dry twigs and found a place on a dry rock to ready a small fire. Savi continued walking and fishing around the pond until she caught seven in all. The largest measured eight inches. After cleaning them, Rico lit the fire and cooked the fish. As usual, they ate every last bit of their meal, leaving only the bones. After dinner Conner took the bones and buried them a reasonable distance away from the camp to ensure the lingering scent of the fish was nowhere near the cave. Once he returned, they all retired to the cave to rehydrate and take a break before preparing their refuge for the evening.

In the cave Savi sat alone, quiet. The others were quiet as well. But Savi wouldn't be quiet for long. This was the night she'd tell her story, one that would deepen their insight into the heart and character of their courageous little friend.

CHAPTER TWENTY-SIX

The group sat in silence for a long time because no one was sure how to begin the conversation. Finally, Rico spoke for the others and started by stating the obvious. "Savi, we need to apologize to you. We were wrong and you were right. You knew what you were doing and where you were going, and we didn't trust you. I'm really sorry for doubting you and adding to your stress out there."

"Me too, Savi," Conner echoed. "I feel like I made things worse for you."

"I'm sorry too. I doubted you and added to the pressure you were already feeling," Jade said, her eyes cast down.

Savi sat quietly with her head bowed and absorbed the words spoken by her weary comrades. Then, as if their apologies were not heard the first time, they tried again.

"Savi, can you forgive us?" Jade pleaded.

"Come on...talk to us," Conner begged.

"Why won't you say anything?" Rico questioned.

Finally, Savi looked up and broke her silence. "You don't have to keep apologizing. It's over. I don't hold anything against you guys because you doubted me. The truth is, I doubted myself. It was the compass I never doubted," she confessed.

"May I show you guys something?" Savi asked.

"Sure," they all agreed.

"What do want to show us?" Jade asked curiously.

"Do me a favor, stand up a minute…come on, do this for me," Savi insisted and waited till they all stood to their feet.

"Now, I want all of you to close your eyes and point in the direction that you think is north." Savi waited as Rico, Jade, and Conner all tried to figure out which way was north, and then point in that direction. After they committed to a direction, she instructed them. "Now stay pointing the way you are, open your eyes, and look at each other."

The three opened their eyes and looked at one another.

"Do you see that you're all pointing in slightly different directions?" she noted. "The compass shows that none of you are actually pointing north. It says north is that way." She lifted her finger and showed them the direction of the compass needle.

Savi now had the others' full attention. "I'll never forget something my dad told me when I was a young girl. He taught me, 'There are two things in this life that will never lie to me, the Bible and a compass.' I've never forgotten those words. Especially today, when I doubted myself, I knew the compass wouldn't lie to me."

Rico, Jade, and Conner sat back down and stared at Savi. Knowing she was the youngest among them, they appeared to be dumbfounded by the maturity of her insights.

Then Jade asked Savi the question that had been on her mind for days. "Savi, we've all talked about why we came on this trip. But, you haven't told us your story. Why did you come to Arrowhead?"

Savi paused before answering. She appeared to reach deep inside for an extra measure of bravery. Then she spoke softly and slowly. "Four months ago, my Uncle Ray accidently killed my five-year-old brother, Joshua," she recalled in a somber tone.

Shocked, Rico interrupted her and blurted out, "What…What do you mean, killed your brother?"

Savi stayed calm and answered, "On April 26 my Uncle Ray came to our house drunk and asked my dad for some money. When my dad refused, he stormed out of the house, got into his car, and backed over my brother Josh who had pulled into the driveway behind him on his bike." She paused as tears rolled down her face. "Josh died in the ambulance on the way to the hospital. And my Uncle Ray was arrested and charged with involuntary manslaughter. He's now serving a six year sentence in a Mississippi prison."

"Oh my God, Savi. That's awful," Jade sobbed. "You must hate your uncle's guts."

Savi looked over at her and again paused for a moment.

"Actually, I finally forgave him recently," she said soberly. "And so has the rest of my family."

Rico, Jade, and Conner all sat quietly with tears brimming and sullen faces listening to Savi's horrific story.

"Forgiving my uncle was the biggest test of my life. At first I hated him like I'd never hated anyone else. Everyone in my family went through a really dark time. But eventually my dad led the way and reminded us of what we knew about forgiveness. He also told us that if we didn't choose to forgive, we'd hurt ourselves in the long run.

Gradually, my heart started to change. It was just three weeks ago that I went with my dad to the prison and saw my Uncle Ray for the first time since the accident. He cried like a baby and accepted full responsibility for his actions. He sobbed like I'd never seen a man cry in my life and begged me to forgive him. He said he'd understand if I never forgave him, but hoped that someday I would. I believed he was sincere and deeply sorry, so I put the palm of my hand up against the glass window that separated us. I told him over the phone that I forgave him. That made him sob even more and then he lifted his hand and placed his palm on the glass over mine.

At that moment, something happened inside of me and my heart softened toward him in a strange way. I looked into his eyes and saw a broken man who would live a lifetime of regret for the foolish mistake he made that cost Josh his life." Savi paused as she tried to fight back her own tears.

"Now, I can answer your question, Jade, about why I came to Arrowhead. My mom and dad thought a change of scenery and some fun might do me some good after the rough season I've been through. And wow, am I having fun out here," she scoffed with her first grin of the evening. "Now let's get everything set up for the night. I've got to believe that there are some berries or mushrooms around here somewhere. That fish didn't even put a dent in my appetite."

Everyone sat quiet for the next minute. Finally, Jade spoke in a serious voice. "Savi, I'll never forget the story you just told us, not for the rest of my life," she admitted.

"Neither will I," Rico affirmed.

"Me either, Savi," Conner added. "Thanks for trusting us enough to tell us such a personal story. And thanks also for forgiving us for what we did to you today. It sucks that we treated you that way."

Feeling somewhat revived despite the story Savi told them, they all got up and began preparations for the night. Jade filled the water bottles and canteens at the pond while Savi gathered pine needles for the cave floor and scoured the area for berries or anything else to eat. Rico and Conner picked up dried branches and twigs for the fire. Afterward, they carved spears to protect the entrance from would be predators in their typical manner.

Fortunately, Savi found some small blackberry bushes near the backside of the pond with a few berries still remaining that had not been eaten by birds or other wildlife. When she brought them back to the cave, everyone wolfed them down in a matter of seconds.

The night revealed a clear starlit sky with a brilliant orange moon rising over the trees from the southeast.

Everyone knew the mountain range was close, but they had not actually seen it yet because of the heavy mist that blanketed the woods all day. Now that night had descended on the forest, it again hid the range from view.

Everyone realized having extended guard shifts was dangerous because they were all so tired. So they decided on one-hour blocks to minimize the possibility of anyone falling asleep on their watch. Savi volunteered for the first shift. In a matter of minutes the others were sound asleep. All was quiet except for the crickets and frogs croaking near the pond. Savi was so tired; she knew she needed to stay on her feet. She figured if she sat down, even for a second, she'd fall asleep in no time. Fortunately, her hour shift passed quickly, which meant it was time to wake up Conner.

When Conner was ready to relieve Savi, he hugged her goodnight and watched as she slipped quietly into the cave. Right before Savi shut her eyes for the night, she looked out of the cave's entrance at the glorious starlit sky. Suddenly, a shooting star appeared. The light trail that followed glowed brightly for a few seconds and then quickly disappeared. Savi glanced over at Conner to see if he had seen the falling star as well. He looked back at her and acknowledged that he had, and for a few moments the two of them grinned at one another in the pale moonlight. Then Savi closed her eyes and drifted off to asleep.

The stars in the sky gradually disappeared as the dark canvass behind them faded into morning light. Soon the moon was barely visible and the birds were beginning to chirp and sing. Jade stood guard on the last shift watching excitedly as the forest around her came alive with sounds and light. Luke had warned them days earlier about the journey over the mountains being slow and difficult, so Jade decided it was time to wake the others. After doing so, she and Savi combed the pond area for more blackberry bushes. They found enough berries to give each of them a couple of hand-fuls. Everyone then drank as much as they could, know-ing the day's trek would be challenging and difficult.

The group packed up quickly and departed from the peaceful refuge and pond that had served them so well. The evening before, Savi had plotted out their course for the day. The route led them in the direction of the mountains toward two possible campsites. One was located at the base of the range and the other near the top of a mountain. Once they arrived at the summit camp, the map indicated they'd be only two and a half miles from the Susquehanna River, which was just a half a mile in front of Camp Arrowhead.

A new sense of hope accompanied the group as they began the day's journey. But they had traveled less than a half-mile when they exited the forest and entered a large clearing. One by one they gasped. Gazing at what stood before them, the hope they carried earlier quickly vanished.

"Luke warned us about this," Savi reminded everyone.

Jade stopped in her tracks, and sat down with her eyes fixed on the mountain range looming in front of her. She began weeping. "There's no way we can make it over those mountains and cross the river in three days," she cried.

Savi bent down and put her hand on Jade's shoulder. "You're right, Jade, because today is August 30 and we only have two days, not three, to cross the river."

CHAPTER TWENTY-SEVEN

Savi's warning that they had only two days to cross the Susquehanna River increased Jade's tears and the sense of hopelessness hovering over the group. The mountains were about a mile and a half before them and looked steep and treacherous. But everyone knew the clock was ticking and there was no time to waste.

"We're not going to get across the river sitting here," Savi exhorted the group. "I know we're all tired, but if we get moving we can probably make the camp near the summit by nightfall."

Luke had marked a few campsite options on the map that they could use depending on how strong they felt. The first was at the base of the mountain they were approaching. The teens knew they needed to keep going, so they set their sights on a second campsite near the top of the mountain.

Though this was an ambitious goal, they had to press forward if they'd have any chance of crossing the river by September 1.

The open terrain and the crisp clear weather made travel much easier than it was the day before. The foursome made steady progress though there were still lots of rocks to climb over. They were encouraged to be gradually getting closer to the mountain range.

"Savi, how long do you guess it will take us to get over these mountains?" Rico asked.

"I'm not sure but the map shows they are high but not too wide. There's a chance we'll be able to see the river when we get to the summit," she answered. "We've got to go a bit west once we pass the first camp spot. Luke said there's a snake trail up the side of the mountain which is a tough climb, but it will save us tons of time."

"We've got no choice," Rico said, resignation lining his voice. "If we don't make it, then we're in real trouble...I won't question your directions anymore, Savi," Rico assured her. "You lead the way and I'll make sure the others keep up." He looked down and around. "Just be sure you keep an eye out for rattlers though. Luke said they like these rocky areas."

"Will do. One bite is enough for me," she said in a serious voice.

The determined group reached the first camp a little after nine, meaning they had the whole day to climb the mountain and reach the camp on the summit. Before attempting the difficult feat, they filled their canteens and water bottles in a gushing stream, no doubt one of a thousand coming down from the jagged mountain peaks above. They also found plenty of berries around to eat and even enough to pack away for later.

After reaching the first camp, they headed west about a quarter mile, walking parallel to the mountains. Eventually, they came upon the snake trail Luke had highlighted on the map. It was narrower than they expected, and worse yet, it hugged the mountain as far as they could see.

"Now I see why Luke said this would slow us down," Jade grumbled. "It will take us forever to get up there."

"Conner, you bring up the rear," Rico instructed. "I'll stay up front between Savi and Jade. We've got to move at a strong pace. Jade, you've got to keep up. Conner, make sure she does."

"That's why I've got this spear," Conner joked.

"Oh, now I'm the problem child," Jade shot back. "Let's see who can't keep up."

"You go, girl!" Conner encouraged.

After a brief break, mostly so they could refresh themselves with some berries and water, they began the grueling task of ascending the mountain. In the beginning the trail was particularly steep and slippery. Over time, however, it flattened out as it zigzagged back and forth across the face of the range. Conversation ceased because each of them needed every breath for the climb.

Savi and Rico watched carefully for snakes as they hiked on what could barely be called a trail. Though they noticed several shed skins from rattlers on the path, none of them saw a live snake all morning, much to their relief. By noon, they had made it nearly halfway up the mountain, and decided to celebrate their not-so-small achievement with a much-needed break.

The view from the side of the mountain was majestic. For the first time they could see the Salmon River again, and the miles of wilderness they had passed through to get to their current location. All of a sudden Jade looked over at Conner. He looked pale and sickly.

"Conner, are you okay?" she asked.

"Uh, no. Not so good," Conner grunted. Suddenly, he started throwing up what little was in his stomach.

"What's going on?" Rico inquired, putting his hand on Conner's back.

Rico waited for Conner to recover a bit and then repeated his question. "What's up, *hot dog*? You okay?"

"Yeah, I'm alright," Conner, acknowledged unconvincingly.

"Come on, man," Rico insisted. "Tell me what's going on?"

"Well, if you must know, heights freak me out…" he confessed in a low voice hoping the girls wouldn't hear. "I looked down a few minutes ago and all of a sudden my head started spinning and I got sick."

"You're afraid of heights? That's nothing to be ashamed of, if you're a girl," Jade teased.

"Jade, that's cruel," Savi responded.

"I'm just playing with him," Jade countered. "He's always kidding with me."

"She's right," Conner agreed. "I guess there'll be no goodnight kiss tonight, huh, Jade?" he joked.

"You must be feeling better…Come on, let's do this," Rico ordered.

Again, they started moving back and forth across the face of the mountain. They were about ten minutes from where they had taken their break when they heard a horrible sound at the base of the mountain. Looking down they saw two animals fighting. Though they were hard to identify from their vantage point, they could see that the one animal was four-legged and light brown like a mountain lion or cougar. It was obviously wounded because it could not run away from the beast stalking it. The other animal appeared to be a huge light-brown bear. Even from half a mile above, they could see that it was enormous. It roared and howled as it moved closer toward its prey. Then with ferocity that chilled them all to the bone, the beast pounced on the animal, killed it, and then began devouring it piece by piece.

Everyone was so terrified and dumbfounded, they just stood and stared at the horrific sight below. No one said a word.

Just then the beast lifted his head and roared. Making the most awful sounds one could imagine, he looked up at the mountains in the direction of the onlookers.

"He spotted us!" Rico cried out. "I know he did. Let's go now!"

Without a moment's hesitation the group moved up along the snake trail as fast as their legs could carry them. No one needed to say it. They all knew they had just seen Vexel for the first time. The hideous monster was probably stalking them and there was no time to spare. Savi estimated at the last break that they had another two miles to reach the summit camp. According to the time they were making, that meant another three hours, and it was now nearly half-past two.

"We've got to get to the camp and fortify the entrance as soon as we can. If Vexel is following us, that's our only chance. God, I wish I had some bullets right now," Savi lamented.

"Even if we had bullets…a pistol wouldn't stop that thing," Rico replied. "Conner, we've got to pick up the pace…we're dead meat out on this trail if Vexel catches us. If we don't get to that camp in a hurry, it's over."

For the next two hours, the group pushed themselves to the limit. Concerned that Vexel was pursuing them up the mountain, they stopped only occasionally for a quick drink. Savi now estimated that they were about an hour away from the camp at the summit.

Exhausted beyond description, the weary travelers finally had to stop for more than a short rest. The air was thinner at this height. They had been on a two-hour forced march, and with the added altitude, they could hardly breathe. After five minutes, Rico decided to look down one last time at the place where they saw Vexel. At their current height, he could barely make out the area, but it was obvious that Vexel was gone. Where he had gone was anyone's guess.

"Okay, let's get to it," Rico commanded. "We've got a ways to go to the summit."

"But I'm so tired," Jade complained.

Rico let the comment pass. Instead, he turned to Savi. "How's your ankle? I noticed you were really limping a few minutes ago."

"It always hurts when I climb," she answered. "But when it's a choice between walk or die…I'm all about walking, no matter how badly it hurts."

"Do you think Vexel's going to catch us?" Jade asked, anxiously.

"If he does," Savi replied. "Conner said he'd eat him for lunch. Remember?"

"Or the other way around," Jade replied in a snarky tone.

"Come on, Jade. Let's walk and save our breath," Savi urged.

The next part of the journey was the hardest of the day. Their energy was waning and the Snake Trail was the steepest since they began their climb. The hope of reaching the camp in sixty minutes was quickly dismissed, as each step grew increasingly difficult. After an hour of hiking, they were still about thirty minutes away from the summit and the camp.

Exhausted, everyone knew they couldn't go on without a break. They all crumbled on the path and reached for their water bottles. The climb had not only taken its toll on them, but it had also nearly depleted their water supply. At this point they had enough, but they all knew they needed to find more water soon.

"I know we're all wiped out, but we only have about a half a mile to go," Savi said between winded breaths. "We've got to keep moving. Come on. Let's go." She struggled back to her feet.

"I need a few more minutes," Jade protested.

"We don't have a few more minutes!" Rico shot back. "We've got to go now if we want to stay alive."

"Okay, okay, help me up," Jade said to Rico. When he did, she whispered in his ear, "You're acting like my drill sergeant not my boyfriend."

"Right now, I am your drill sergeant," Rico replied. He kissed her gently on the cheek and added, "Sorry, but my first priority is keeping us all alive. Let's get moving."

The predicted final half hour to the summit camp turned out to be only twenty-minutes.

When they arrived, they found the place to be all they could have hoped for. A narrow entrance to the cave made it relatively easy to fortify, and the depth of it gave them plenty of room for sleeping. A small creek flowed on the eastern side of the cave about fifty feet away, and just as important, several luscious clusters of berries hung delicately on the branches of some nearby bushes.

Rico and Conner immediately worked to secure the cave's entrance while Savi and Jade refilled the canteen and water bottles, picked berries, and gathered pine needles to insulate themselves from the cold ground in the cave. Once all the preparations were done, they all sat down behind the sharpened wood stakes now guarding the entrance. Rico and Conner placed more than the usual number of stakes at the entrance, knowing they might need added protection if their greatest fears were realized.

The sun had barely set when to their horror, they heard crackling sounds in the trees nearby. Rico hushed everyone and they all peered outside in the direction of the noise. Again, branches snapped, but they couldn't see anything yet.

Visibly shaken, Jade whispered the obvious question. "Do you think it's Vexel?"

CHAPTER TWENTY-EIGHT

They detected movement in the woods across the small clearing. Raising their spears and knives they prepared themselves for what was surely the ultimate showdown. All of a sudden, a slender, tall figure emerged from the darkened woods.

"Luke!" Savi shouted.

"Is that you, missy?" he replied.

Everyone quickly dismantled the barrier they had constructed and rushed to Luke. The girls hugged him, and the boys shook his hand and exchanged chest bumps. They all told him how happy they were to see him and sighed in relief that he was all right.

"Luke, I can't believe it. We thought you might be dead," Jade admitted. "We heard two gunshots and then nothing."

"Well, rumors about my demise are obviously false," Luke boasted. "And about those shots—a man has to eat, doesn't he? I had a clean shot at a deer and I took it. The second shot was to put him out of his misery."

"How did you find us again?" Savi asked.

"I came across your tracks on the Snake Trail," Luke explained. "Earlier in the morning Vexel doubled back on me. He somehow got behind me so I needed to get some elevation and distance between us. I followed you guys up the trail to ensure he wouldn't come after you. The high vantage point helped me to have a bird's eye view of everything. That's when I saw him at the base of the mountain killing that big cat. I had him in my sights for a second, but he dragged the mountain lion away behind some rocks and I lost sight of him. I also knew if I missed him, it would give away my position."

"We saw him too," Conner affirmed. "He was eating an animal down below. You say it was a big cat?"

"Yeah, a mountain lion," Luke replied. "There are plenty of them in these parts. He must have gotten in a scuffle earlier in the morning with another cat and been wounded. Usually those fights are over a female. Vexel must have smelled the blood, tracked him down, and finished him off."

"Luke, are you sure that was Vexel?" Savi asked.

"Oh, that was Vexel alright," Luke, confirmed. "And he's not only vicious, but he's also smart. Like I said, he doubled back on me this morning. Thank God he found that injured mountain lion to distract him. That bought us all some time."

"Why are you so sure that was Vexel?" Savi questioned him a second time.

"Because I got a good glimpse of him," Luke replied. "And now I know the rumors are true."

"What rumors are you talking about?" Rico wondered aloud.

"Rumors about the fire and the bear…"

"Go on," he insisted.

"About ten years ago, there was a pretty devastating fire south of here. Acres of forest were destroyed and hundreds of animals were trapped in the blaze and killed. There was a rumor that a huge grizzly bear got trapped under a burning tree that fell on him. Somehow the bear managed to survive, but was disfigured due to the burns covering much of his body. I saw him from a distance today, but close enough to confirm that Vexel is that same bear. He's the ugliest beast I've ever seen, and tall. About twelve feet on his hind legs, if I'm guessing right, and with a five-foot shoulder span. I'll bet he's close to a thousand pounds. Much bigger than any Idaho grizzly I've ever seen, so he must be a coastal transplant."

Savi interrupted. "What do you mean a coastal transplant?"

"My dad told me that twelve years ago, the forest service relocated some bears from the West Coast—specifically, Washington State near the Canadian border. They moved them here to thin out the grizzly population on the coast. Vexel has to be one of those bears," Luke surmised.

"So did he start killing people after the fire?" Conner inquired.

"Oh no, he killed the first person before that. Most people thought he died in that fire, but about six months later the killings started up again. At first he just went after animals, then he started killing people like he had before. Once a grizzly has tasted human blood they never forget it. These kinds of bears have to be hunted and killed, or they will keep on killing people indiscriminately…just like he killed my father," Luke said emphatically.

"Do you think he followed us up the Snake Trail?" Savi asked Luke.

"No, not right away…I stopped about halfway up on the trail and waited for several minutes to see if he was following. He never showed up. But that doesn't mean much. That trail is not the only way for a bear to get up the mountain."

"What do you mean?" Jade asked.

"I mean that a bear doesn't need a snake trail to get up the mountain," Luke said in a matter of fact tone. "He just climbs right up."

Jade let out a nervous breath and then asked. "Do you think we should stay here tonight? I'm not feeling too safe in this cave anymore."

"I suggest you all get a good night's sleep," Luke replied. "I'm well rested, and I'll keep watch for as long as I can tonight. You all are probably exhausted and need some sleep. By sundown tomorrow, you've got to try to get across the river. The dam releases water into the Susquehanna the day after tomorrow. There's no telling what time they'll open it up…If you get caught on the river when it opens, you haven't got a prayer," Luke warned them solemnly. He paused a moment, and then added, "There's one final thing that might help you sleep a little better. When I killed that deer I cut out its liver and some of the other organs. I packed them in plastic bags then sealed the bags in two more plastic bags to mask the smell."

"That's so gross," Jade complained. "And you said that would help us sleep better?"

"Well, yes. Because on my way up here I planted some of that stuff around to keep him distracted and hopefully away from us for the time being. I've got a few more parts here in these plastic bags if you'd like to see them." Luke reached for his pack.

"Um, no," Jade said as politely as possible. "I don't know about the rest of these guys, but I'll pass on that if you don't mind."

"No problem," Luke smirked. "I'll just keep these gizzards for Vexel and me. They're nice to have around if you get really hungry you know."

Jade's normally fair complexion turned a slight shade of green. She scooted away as quickly as possible, fearing that Luke might pull something else out of his backpack that she'd rather not see.

After Jade excused herself, Savi asked Luke if he'd give her one of the plastic bags filled with the deer's internal organs. She told him that she wanted to have it just in case they ever got into a jam. Luke agreed and gave her one of the plastic bags that she tucked in her backpack.

The security of knowing Luke was standing guard gave everyone a true but unfamiliar sense of safety. This feeling, coupled with their exhaustion from the hard day's march up the mountain, made going to sleep that much easier.

Luke stayed up and watched nearly the whole night before finally waking Rico at four in the morning. Then Luke slept for about an hour while Rico stood guard.

At morning light, Rico woke everyone and encouraged them to pack up so they could start moving again. Before they left the cave, Luke gave them each a strip of jerky that they ate along with some of the berries they found the day before. He also traded his machete with Rico for the empty pistol he had given him days earlier.

"Okay, listen up," Luke told them. "There are some things you should know before you leave here…It's a steep decline down the mountain. And the Snake Trail ends about halfway down. I showed Savi one last cave on the map, in case you need it. But I hope you don't. Try to get to the river as quickly as you can. It's about a quarter mile swim across it. Once you're on the other side, Camp Arrowhead is within a half mile."

He turned in Conner and Jade's direction. "You guys fill all the containers with water from the stream and collect a day's supply of berries. Savi and Rico bring the map and come with me. Let me show you where you're headed."

Conner and Jade began doing as Luke had instructed. Luke grabbed all his gear, and Savi and Rico followed him up a small path that ascended sharply past the cave. They hiked up a steep incline for about ten minutes with Luke in the lead, when all at once he stopped. Savi reached Luke first, followed by Rico close behind. They gasped in amazement as they took in a magnificent panoramic view of the valley below, now visible from the top of the mountain. From this majestic viewpoint, they could see the steep decline of the mountain Luke had spoken about earlier. They also saw the emerald green forest in the distance, and best of all, their first glimpse of the turquoise Susquehanna River.

Luke pointed in the direction of Camp Arrowhead, though it wasn't visible from their vantage point. "That's where you're headed." He took a step forward and leaned over the edge. "It's going to take you the better part of the day to get down this mountain. Once you do, you'll be about a mile and a half from the river. Savi, let me see the map."

Luke pointed at the spot where they were, then moved his finger northward. "Look here. If for any reason you need it, there's a safe cave less than an eighth of a mile from the river."

Then Luke stood upright, and motioned for Savi and Rico to come closer. He pointed toward the Susquehanna and said, "Do you see the small sandy beach on the other side of the river?"

"Yes," they replied in unison.

"Well, directly across from that in the river there's a good-sized sandbar," Luke continued. "When you're crossing the river, that's a good place to take a break if you need one. Once you get on the other side, Camp Arrowhead is straight ahead through the forest about half of a mile. Before I go, there's one last thing. Watch out for mountain lions. There are a lot of them up here. It's mating season and they're edgy. If you surprise one or catch 'em hungry, they'll attack you without hesitation," he warned.

Savi and Rico looked at one another, but didn't say anything.

"I've got to go now," Luke decreed in a determined voice. "I've never been so close to getting Vexel, and I'm not letting him get away."

"You're leaving?" Savi asked.

"Yeah, it's time for me to go," Luke acknowledged. "You've got a rough road ahead of you," he cautioned them. "It's obvious to me that you two are the strong ones in the group. So get Jade, Conner, and yourselves back to Arrowhead safely. I probably won't see you again, so be careful…and God bless."

Luke extended his hand for Rico to shake. Luke then gave Savi a parting hug. The two of them again thanked him for everything he had done.

Savi sobbed as she wrapped her arms around Luke a second time and said good-bye. "I'll never forget you, Luke. For as long as I live…I'll always be grateful to you. All of us owe you our lives," she said appreciatively through her tears. "Promise me you'll be extra careful…Remember, you told us Vexel is smart. So you be smarter." Savi then reached in her vest pocket and took out her small Bible. She quickly thumbed through the pages until she got to Psalm 23, then she tore the page from the book and handed it to Luke.

"Luke, I have nothing to give you but this. I hope you find comfort in it…God bless and keep you," she said through her tears.

Then tears welled up in Luke's eyes.

"No one's done or said anything this kind to me in a long time, missy. I promise I won't forget you either. Go…before I start bawling. You guys have a big day ahead of you."

Savi and Rico watched as Luke descended the mountain, entered a grove of pine trees, and then disappeared. Once he was out of sight, they quickly made their way back to camp and reconnected with Jade and Conner who were waiting inside the cave. Together they had already filled the canteens and water bottles and also picked enough berries to sustain them for at least a day.

After they gathered their belongings, the others followed Savi up a steep path to the trail that Luke had marked out on the map. Again, his warning about the steep descent proved accurate. The Snake Trail was narrow and difficult, and as a precaution, the group tied a rope to each other in case one of them fell.

Savi led the way, followed by Jade, Conner, and Rico. Conner's fear of heights came into play at every turn. He hugged the mountain wall and refused to look down, while at the same time he kept his eyes on Jade's back as he put one foot in front of the other. More than once, Rico's only recourse was to pull Conner along on the rope connecting the two of them.

"Conner, I won't let you fall," Rico assured him. He turned back and glanced at his terrified face, then added, "Chico's got you covered, *hot dog*, just follow me."

Conner locked eyes with Rico and tried to muster up a smile, but he was too afraid, and his face wouldn't cooperate.

Up front, Savi and Jade moved along the trail at a reasonable pace, though they felt the rope tighten from time to time, signaling Conner's resistance. Suddenly,

Savi stopped dead in her tracks. Everyone could tell something was wrong.

"Savi, what's wrong?" Jade asked anxiously.

Savi was white as a sheet and could do nothing but point. Jade looked in the direction Savi had pointed and then let out a blood-curdling scream.

CHAPTER TWENTY-NINE

S tartled by Jade's scream, Rico moved ahead of her
to see what was going on. A large rattlesnake was
perched on a rock about ten feet in front of Savi. Its
tail was making the unmistakable sound that Savi had
heard too late once before. Rico quickly moved the girls
back behind him and unclipped himself from the rope.
Using his spear he carefully inched toward the venomous creature. The snake's head rose…ready to strike.

Rico poked and teased the rattler with his spear in
an attempt to get it to lunge at him. Sure enough, it did.
Both girls screamed as the snake sprang toward Rico.
He then used the tip of his spear to swat the rattler off
the rock and onto the trail. Again, the agitated snake
raised its head at the approaching spear. For a second
time it lurched violently at Rico. This time it landed a
couple feet short of him, and he immediately swung his
spear tip across the path and knocked the rattler several
feet down the side of the mountain.

Since the snake was no longer a threat, Rico forced
the girls and Conner past the spot where it had been
and down the trail about fifty feet. Once there, they
stopped and took some time to regroup.

"What else can happen to us?" an exasperated Jade yelled. "Savi, are you okay?"

"Now I am," she sighed.

After a careful inspection of the area, Savi sat down on a rock to catch her breath. She looked over at Rico with a sense of relief and sincere appreciation. "Thanks...I don't think I could have done that without you."

"Sure you could. You just didn't need to," he assured her.

"No really, Rico, I couldn't have done that...Not after just getting bitten," she insisted.

"Well, that's what friends are for," he replied.

Then he looked over at Conner, "How about you, Conner? You doing alright?"

"Yeah, I'm surviving," he replied. "Let's just get off this mountain."

Without another word, Rico reattached himself to the rope and headed back down the trail with the others in tow. A short time later they deemed it safe enough to untie the rope and walk freely.

Before long, they were halfway down the mountain. Unfortunately, they could see the snake trail was about to end. They decided to use the rope again to reconnect themselves to one another, and after a short break, continued along the rocky path.

Once the trail ended, the trek down the mountain was much more challenging and difficult. Savi led them down the steepest part of the mountain by moving from one tree to the next. From time to time one of them would fall and slow their descent. These delays made their trip wearisome and more than a little frustrating.

By noon they were about two-thirds of the way down from the summit. Though the altitude became less of an issue the lower they went, it still took something out of them, and they all wanted to stop and take another break. Unfortunately, what they couldn't stop was time. The relentless ticking of the clock hung over them like a dark cloud, so they decided to keep on going.

"Savi, at this pace, do you think we'll make it to the river by the end of the day?"

"I don't know" she replied. "But I'm pretty sure it won't be long before we find out…Come on, let's get off this mountain."

Eventually, they noticed the mountain began to flatten out and the decline decreased significantly. The roped team was finally able to untie themselves and hike normally for the first time in quite a while. This new freedom allowed them to move much faster down the remaining part of the mountain.

Finally, the exhausted hikers realized they had finally reached bottom. It was now three o'clock in the afternoon and the weary group found comfort in their accomplishment, and in the fact that they were getting closer to safety all the time. According to the map, they were just one-and-a-half miles from the Susquehanna River. That meant that they were only a little over two miles from Camp Arrowhead.

"We're on the home stretch now," Savi crowed. "I can almost see the finish line from here."

"I need a break," Jade lamented. "I'm wiped out."

"Rico, we both need a break," Savi added. "Let's stop for a few minutes. I need something to eat."

"Me too," Rico agreed.

The tired foursome sat together and surveyed the mountain they had just descended. After rehydrating themselves and finishing the remaining berries, they lay down on the ground and enjoyed an extended rest.

"Conner, you must be feeling better, huh?" Savi asked.

"Are you kidding me? I puked so many times up there, I lost count," he complained. "No one said anything in the camp brochure about mountain climbing."

"Speaking of Camp Arrowhead, they must think we're all dead," Jade snickered. "Are they going to be surprised when they see us."

"I'm sad about what our parents and family must be going through," Savi lamented. "They've probably cried their eyes out by now."

"My parents are probably happy they don't have to pay for my college," Jade grumbled.

Savi folded her arms. "Jade, that's not true. They're probably sick with worry."

"It looks like I may actually find out…Honestly though, I doubted we'd make it until now," Jade admitted.

"Okay, let's get moving. I've got this creepy feeling that Vexel is following us," Rico confided. "We've got to get to the river before dark."

The group journeyed over the flat terrain toward the river. Savi made several course corrections as they hiked. By 3:45 p.m. they were less than a quarter mile from the Susquehanna. Tired, they decide to stop one last time for a quick break before completing the final leg to the river. They sat within talking distance of one another and rested near a large cluster of big rocks. Once they were settled in, they quickly drank the last of their water.

"I'm guessing twenty minutes to the river," Savi exclaimed excitedly.

"Can you believe it?" Conner said. "We've come such a long way since that rafting accident."

"What's the first thing you're going to do when you get back to Arrowhead?" Savi asked Jade. Before she could answer, they both saw something move behind Conner.

Terrified, both girls jumped up...When a mountain lion stepped out of the woods, they both screamed. It had snuck up on them and was now perched on a rock several feet away, directly above where Conner was sitting.

"Nobody move," Rico hollered as he slowly reached for his spear. Conner had his back to the danger and had no idea what was happening. Startled, he reached for his spear. When he did, the large cat leapt from the rock onto him.

Rico immediately jumped to his feet and charged the mountain lion that was now mauling Conner's arm. Conner was doing his best to fight back, but to no avail.

Rico plunged his spear into the hindquarter of the vicious cat and wounded it. All of a sudden, the injured beast turned on him. Savi ran toward Conner and grabbed his spear while Jade cowered and screamed in terror behind a small pine tree.

The mountain lion quickly overtook Rico and tossed him to the ground, clamping his jaw on Rico's lower leg. In a desperate move, Savi lurched forward and drove Conner's spear into the lion's side. The animal shook violently and fell bleeding onto the ground. It writhed wildly, giving Savi time to grab Rico's spear. With all the strength she could muster, she plunged its sharpened point into the downed lion and killed it.

Savi quickly looked at Conner screaming in pain and realized his arm was a bloody mess. Despite Conner's cries, it was obvious to her that Rico was hurt worse. His lower leg was punctured with nasty bites and bleeding badly. Rico was on the ground moaning and groaning and grabbing at his wounded leg.

"Jade, hurry!" Savi shouted. "Get the medical kit out of my pack."

"Rico, just hold on," she pleaded. "The mountain lion is dead. Just listen to my voice and stay with me."

Jade quickly handed the medical kit to Savi, and she took out the last two rolls of gauze, three large bandages, and an Ace bandage for wrapping the wound. "Here, go help Conner." She gave her the gauze and bandages.

"Rico! Stay awake and look at me..." His eyes opened a little. "That's it. Now listen to me. Your calf is damaged pretty badly. I need you to bite on this." She handed him a short thick stick. "I've got to close the wound and it's going to hurt. Do you understand?"

Rico could only nod at her. She shoved the stick in his mouth and began working on the wound. Before attempting to close it, she removed his belt and used it as a tourniquet to slow the flow of blood. He bit hard on the stick and winced in pain as Savi pinched the wounds closed and bandaged it tightly in an attempt to stop the bleeding.

Meanwhile, Jade tried to calm Conner down, so she could treat his wound. He was hysterical and screaming uncontrollably.

"Savi, what do I do?" Jade yelled.

"Come over here and finish putting this on Rico's leg," she commanded.

Savi then left Rico and rushed to Conner. She grabbed him by the vest and shook him.

"Conner! Conner! We can't help you unless you stop," Savi exhorted. "I know you're hurting but you've got to let us help you"

"My arm…it hurts so bad," Conner moaned.

"I know, now let me help you."

"Savi!" Jade screamed. "Rico's going to sleep."

"Then don't let him," Savi shouted back. "You've got to keep him awake. I'll be right there."

Savi quickly wrapped Conner's arm and slowed the bleeding. Then she hurried back to Rico's side.

"You go stay with Conner while I work on Rico," Savi ordered.

"Is he going to die, Savi?" Jade asked in a panic.

"Not on my watch. Now get over there and tend to Conner…Now, Jade!"

The chaotic scene gradually calmed down. Savi bandaged both Rico and Conner's injuries, and after nearly an hour, their wounds had all but stopped bleeding. Savi used every resource at her disposal to steady them both. Conner had finally quieted down, though he still suffered terribly. On the other hand, Rico's leg wound was deeper and more severe. The mountain lion had clamped down on his right calf and dug his fangs in deep around his lower leg. He also had several scratch marks on his chest from the cat's claws. Though still in a lot of pain, he appeared to be stabilized.

"What now, Savi?" Jade blurted in a panicked voice.

"We slow down and figure out what to do," Savi replied calmly. "Jade, I need you to pull it together right now...I need your help, and so do they. You're going to have to toughen up and quit freaking out on me. We've got big problems here, and I don't need to add you to the list. Got it?"

Savi turned away and brushed back a tear.

"Sorry," Jade apologized. "I live in San Francisco. I don't see this kind of stuff every day."

Savi dried her eyes.

"I get it, Jade. Do you think we fight animals in the streets of Mississippi? This is overwhelming for me too...But we've got to keep it together, or we're all going to die out here."

"You're right. But please don't yell at me, Savi...I'm just really scared." Jade did her best to compose herself. "What can I do to help?"

"Go check on Conner," Savi replied. "And stop asking me questions for a while, Okay?"

Jade went to check on Conner while Savi worked on Rico's wounds. Finally, the bleeding had stopped and he was sitting up and leaning against a rock.

"I'll bet that hurt worse than my snake bite," Savi said to Rico with a smirk.

"You wouldn't believe it…I've never felt anything so painful before," he admitted as he winced, "I can't believe you killed that mountain lion, Savi."

"Well, I didn't have a lot of choice. You guys were lying around whining like junior high girls after a break up," Savi joked. "Somebody had to do something."

Rico forced a smile for the first time since the attack.

"Hey, I need you to do me a favor," Savi said. "Tell your girlfriend to get it together. She's driving me crazy."

"You know she's just scared," Rico grunted as he looked down at his bloody leg and twitched in pain. "I don't think I can walk on this, let alone get us to the river in time. It's already almost six o'clock."

Then he looked Savi directly in the eyes. "I think you need to leave me here…and save yourselves…I can't go any further."

CHAPTER THIRTY

Rico's request to be left behind infuriated Savi. She gave him an angry look and replied, "Are you kidding me? No one is getting left out here alone…Especially you."

Realizing what she had just said, she quickly tried to cover her tracks. "I mean…you've gotten us all this way. I would never leave you out here. No chance," she insisted emphatically.

"I haven't gotten us here alone, Savi…Oh God, my leg's killing me—It was as much you as me," he affirmed.

"Whatever, but I'm not leaving you behind," she said resolutely. "My dad was in the army, and he taught me that you never leave a wounded soldier on the battlefield. Either you come with us or we all stay here."

"Can Conner walk?" Rico asked.

"I'm sure he can. The lion bit him on the arm, not the leg," she told him.

"Okay, help me up," Rico asked. "Let's see if I can put any weight on my leg."

Savi helped Rico to his feet. He discovered his leg was damaged so badly that he couldn't stand or hardly put any pressure on it. Once it became evident that he couldn't walk without assistance, Savi decided to try something. She retrieved the bloody spear from the side of the fallen beast and handed it to Rico.

"Try using this like a cane and see if that helps," Savi suggested.

Rico tried her suggestion and discovered he could hobble forward by using the spear.

"Okay, let me help you sit back down, and then I'll go and get Conner ready," Savi told him.

When Savi returned to Conner, Jade immediately went back to Rico.

"Are you alright? I thought that the mountain lion was going to kill you," Jade said through tears. "I didn't know what to do to help you."

"Hey, you couldn't do anything about that, but you can do something now."

"What?" Jade asked.

"You've got to help Savi," he said to her. "Do whatever she says. She's the one that's going to lead us out of here. Promise me you'll suck it up and help her, Jade."

"I will, Rico," Jade promised. "I already told her that."

A sobering thought popped into Savi's head. She looked around and saw that there was blood everywhere. She remembered that Vexel was attracted by the smell of it and insisted they had to leave the place immediately. Conner stood for the first time and realized he could walk fine despite the burning pain in his arm.

Savi returned to Rico and Jade and told them that they were leaving right away. She instructed them to bring only Conner's spear, their knives, the rope, and whatever was important that they could carry in their vest pockets, nothing else. Before leaving, she reached into her backpack and pulled out the plastic bag Luke had given her and stuffed it in her back vest pocket.

"Why do you need that?" Jade asked, curiously.

"You never know. We might need it in a pinch to distract Vexel," Savi replied.

Once everyone was ready, Savi checked the map and compass and pointed in the direction they should go.

"Jade, you're way taller. So you help Rico. He'll have to lean on you along with the cane. Make sure you tell me if he starts bleeding again," she cautioned. "Conner, you come here and walk up front with me."

"Okay, we'll try to keep up," Jade assured her. "Savi, you've got to go slow. Rico won't be able to move very fast," she added.

"Yeah, I know. I'll keep an eye on you guys," Savi assured her.

The girls guided the wounded boys slowly through the remaining wilderness. They had to stop every few hundred feet for Rico to catch his breath. The agonizing journey over the last quarter mile to the river seemed to take forever.

Savi realized it was now 9:30 at night on August 31. The dam was going to open the next day, maybe by early morning, but there was no way they could get across the river in the dark. Without some kind of assistance neither Rico nor Conner could make the quarter mile they needed to swim.

After hours of struggle through the dark woods, Savi heard the gurgling of the river. Rico and Conner had been moaning in pain for the last hour. Both of them were bleeding again and the girls were exhausted by the difficult trek and from helping the boys. Finally, Savi and Conner hiked over a small incline and there it was before them, the Susquehanna River. Completely spent, they all collapsed on the ground. Savi dragged herself up and went to the river's edge to refill the canteens and water bottles they had packed in their vests.

"Here, drink as much as you want. There's a river full out there," Savi said to Rico and Conner.

Savi tossed Jade a water bottle. Then she downed her whole canteen. When she finished she turned to Jade. "You did good. I'm really proud of you. I couldn't have gotten them both here by myself."

"Thanks for saying that," Jade said. "I know you said I shouldn't ask you questions, but Rico's bleeding again. Is there anything we can do to stop it?"

"I'll go check on him," Savi replied. "And Jade…the question thing… it was a bit stressful back there. I just meant at the scene of the attack. You can ask me whatever you'd like now, Okay?"

"Well…I wasn't sure if you meant ever…" Jade replied.

"You know better than that," Savi replied. "Now go and refill the water bottles. Make sure these guys get plenty to drink. I'll go and tend to Rico."

Savi removed the blood-soaked gauze from Rico's calf. Since they were now out of clean gauze, she washed it in the river. She also used the last drops of the peroxide on his wound. After trying her best to dry off the gauze, she rewrapped Rico's wound. Then Savi turned to Conner to inspect his injuries.

"How are you doing big guy? That was quite a nasty bite." Savi examined Conner's arm.

"You mean when I bit the mountain lion?" he quipped.

"You are feeling better already," Savi countered with a grin.

"Not really. My arm is killing me..." He looked over his shoulder. "How's Rico doing? How bad is his leg?" Conner asked.

"It's pretty bad. He won't be playing football for a while. Or walking, for that matter," she added.

Savi looked on the map and saw where Luke had circled a cave that looked to be a few hundred yards away from their current location. She informed the others that it was too dangerous for them to stay out in the open all night, and against their protests, told them she was going off alone to try to find the cave. No one was strong enough to resist or could have stopped her anyway, so off she went, hunting for the much-needed refuge.

Within a few minutes she found the cave and headed back to tell the others. Once she was reunited with them, she roused them to their feet, and together they made the short but painful journey through the dark woods back to the cave.

"Jade, help me gather some pine needles for the guys to lie on. We'd better get a few minutes of rest as well. Then we'll fortify the entrance."

"You got it," Jade replied.

Once they finished gathering the pine needles, the girls dragged some downed branches over to the cave's entrance to use as stakes against predators. When all the preparations were done, Savi and Jade collapsed in a heap next to Rico and Conner now sleeping on the floor of their new refuge.

"You said I could ask you questions again," Jade blurted out. "So here's one. What are we going to do?"

"I'm not sure yet," Savi replied. "I need a few minutes of quiet time to pray and think."

"Well, when you're ready, let me know what you think."

"I will," Savi promised.

Jade laid down and in the next few minutes was fast asleep with the others.

Savi stood alone at the entrance to the cave and looked up at a nearly full moon and a myriad of glimmering stars. Then she looked down at her friends and bowed her head for the longest time. Every few minutes either Rico or Conner winced in pain and let out a painful cry before falling back to sleep. The constant moaning and groaning was awful to hear. Savi stood by herself and prayed for help and guidance.

Like the others, Savi was beat. But she realized she needed to stay awake, or risk another attack from a predator. After standing watch for a while, she pulled out her Bible and her little flashlight, hoping to find some words of inspiration. She thumbed through the pages until her eyes fell on a verse she had never read before. "Greater love has no one than this, that he lay down his life for his friends." She closed the book and for the next hour pondered the words she had read. Then she woke Jade to take the next shift.

Once Jade was ready to relieve Savi, she asked her again, "Did you think of a plan?"

"Yes, I've got one," Savi told her, "but you're going to have to be brave and strong to help me make it work."

She cocked her head to one side. "What do you mean…I'm going to have to be brave and strong?"

"Just what I said, brave and strong. We're going to use the rope I brought with me and the machete Luke gave to Rico to make a small raft for Rico to lie on. First thing in the morning, we're going to have to kick as hard as we can to get the raft across the river before the dam opens. Once we get to the other side we'll be just a half-mile from Camp Arrowhead. Can you do that, Jade?"

"Yeah, I can do that. It sounds like our only option… I can't believe you thought of that on your own."

Savi smiled. "I didn't…I had some help," she replied, as she looked heavenward. "I'm going to get some sleep. At first light, whoever is on watch will wake the other and we'll build the raft. Let the guys sleep as long as they can."

Other than the occasional moans and cries of Rico and Conner, the night passed quietly. Jade had the last watch before the sun appeared above the horizon. As soon as it was light, she woke up Savi. The two of them used the machete to cut similar length pine and fir boughs about five feet long and four inches in diameter. Then they cut three lengths of pine to tie across the bottom of the raft to stabilize the timber and keep it flat. Savi knew that the fir branches were particularly buoyant and useful to help the raft float with Rico's added weight on it. Again, using the machete, Savi trimmed the branches so they would fit tightly next to one another. Then she tied them together firmly with freshly cut pieces of rope and finished constructing the makeshift ark.

With much difficulty, the girls dragged the raft to the river's edge. Then they returned to the cave to wake the boys. After a quick breakfast of water and berries, Savi told them about her plan. Rico was too weak to argue and Conner's arm was bleeding again. He tried his best not to show it, but his arm was killing him. Carefully, the girls helped the boys to their feet. Before leaving, Savi made sure everyone drank a little more water as a precaution.

Just as they grabbed hold of their crude raft, they heard the horrific sounds of a bear growling. Then it let out one loud roar. It sounded as if it was less than a quarter mile away. The terrifying noises left little doubt in anyone's mind what they were hearing…It was Vexel!

CHAPTER THIRTY-ONE

Savi realized the horrific sounds they just heard meant Vexel was only about a quarter mile away. There was no time to waste. Hurriedly but cautiously, Savi and Jade helped Rico and Conner out of the cave. This took great effort on their part since they were both badly hurt and in great pain. The journey from the cave to the river's edge would be difficult, to say the least.

"Savi, I can't!" Rico moaned, then he fell to the ground in agony after only a few steps. "My leg feels worse today than it did yesterday…You've got to leave me so you can get to the river…Vexel's close and the dam is about to open. Go…please!"

"You get your butt up right now and man-up!" Savi screamed. "I told you…I'm not leaving you!" She grabbed his arm and pulled him up with a sudden, forceful jerk.

"We've got to go, Savi!" Conner shouted. "Vexel's right behind us."

"You and Jade get to the river," Savi ordered. "Start dragging the raft up the shore as far as you can. Once we launch it, the current will grab it and pull it downstream. We've got to make sure we angle the raft upriver toward the other shore, or we'll get swept downstream. Now go…hurry!" she commanded. "I'll follow with Rico."

"We can't leave…" Jade started to say.

Savi interrupted her. "You do what I said and go now! Or we are all going to die. Got it?"

Reluctantly, Jade and Conner left Savi and Rico and headed toward the river to find the raft. The going was slow because Conner was in such pain. Jade had to constantly help him along the way.

"Slow down," Conner pleaded. "I can't go that fast. My arm feels like it's on fire."

"We've got to hurry," Jade said between breaths. "Without you, I can't move the raft."

"No way I can pull that thing," he protested. "It's too heavy."

After the difficult trek through the woods, they eventually found the raft on the shore where the girls had left it earlier. Jade tried moving the raft on her own, but with little success. Conner lay on the shore moaning in pain and nursing his wounds.

Jade turned and shot a glare in his direction. "Please, Conner…You've got to help me. I can't do this by myself."

"I can't."

She went over to him and pulled on his good arm. "Come on, I'll help you up. We've got to hurry and get this raft further up the shore or we're all dead."

Savi and Rico were far behind, but were slowly making their way toward the river. Rico didn't have enough strength to use his spear as a cane any longer, so after it fell to the ground for the third time, Savi decided to leave it. Rico now leaned hard against Savi's petite frame, and she found herself almost having to carry him. This made the journey extremely slow and difficult for both of them.

"Rico, we're almost there…you can do it," she said in an encouraging tone. "Just hold on to me and use your good leg."

"I'm trying. I'm trying…It hurts so bad. I've got to stop for a minute," he begged her.

"No. We've got to keep going…Look at me…the river is right there through the trees. You can see it now. It's only a hundred feet away."

Rico stopped. "I'll never make it. Just let go of me, please Savi."

"Listen, I can't carry you and argue at the same time," she yelled at him. "Now shut up and walk, or I'll slap you like I did Jade. Got it?"

"Okay…I'll try." He drew in a deep breath and pushed forward.

After some more agonizing steps they were now just fifty feet from the river. Then, without warning, Rico fell.

Savi shook him as he lay on the ground. "Rico, you've got to get up. The raft's right there."

"I'm done, Savi," he said resolutely. Both eyes closed. "I can't…It's over."

"Oh, no it's not," Savi, shouted. She reached down and squeezed the wound on his calf. Rico yelled out as loud as Savi had ever heard him. He looked at her with anger, followed by a flurry of obscenities.

"Get up right now, or I'll squeeze it again," she threatened as she pulled Rico up on one knee.

"I hate you, Savi!" Rico shouted at her.

"I hate you too," she shot back. "Now get your butt up!"

Somehow, Savi managed to get Rico back on his feet despite his protests, and got him moving again. She had her arms firmly wrapped around Rico's waist, though they moved at a snail's pace, but at least they were moving. Finally, they reached the shore. When they did, they both fell hard to the ground, she exhausted, he in agony.

Meanwhile, Jade and Conner had managed to drag the raft nearly a hundred yards upstream. They too were lying on the shore thoroughly spent.

Just then, Vexel let out a bone-chilling roar. Seeing that Savi needed her help to move Rico, Jade ran as fast as she could down the shore toward them. The two girls pulled Rico to his feet and started walking, and at times dragging him, up the riverbank in the direction of the raft. He yelled in pain with every step. After a couple minutes of hard work, the girls finally got him to the raft. Concerned that Vexel would break out of the woods at any moment, the girls dragged the raft from the shore halfway into the water. Then they carefully sat Rico on it and helped him lie down on his back. His agonizing cries were awful to listen to as they moved him.

The raft now sat low in the water because of Rico's weight, though it stayed afloat enough to keep his head above the water line.

Another terrifying roar echoed through the trees, except this time it sounded closer. Suddenly, the verse Savi read out of her Bible the night before flashed through her mind. In an instant, she knew what she had to do. The only way to rescue her friends was to distract Vexel and lay down her life to save her friends. If she could convince the beast to come after her, they might have time to get away.

"Quick, Jade, you and Conner get Rico across the river," Savi ordered. "You'll have to kick hard, or you won't reach the opposite shore…Conner, use your good arm to hold onto the raft, but you've got to hurry. Vexel's close and the dam could open at any minute." Savi gave the raft a push. "Now go!"

Jade and Conner did as instructed and started kicking and moving the raft away from the shore. When Jade turned back, she realized that Savi had disappeared.

"Savi!" Jade screamed. "Where are you?"

Without Savi, Jade and Conner were confused about what to do next.

"We can't leave her alone!" Rico shouted. "We've got to go back."

"We can't go back or we'll all die!" Conner yelled back at Rico.

"Savi said she's coming. We've got to keep moving. That's what she told us to do," Conner shouted emphatically.

"He's right," Jade said. "She said she'd follow right behind us."

"I don't care what she said," Rico barked. "We've got to turn back and get her." He leaned back toward the shore they had just left, almost tipping over the raft in the process.

"Lay down, Rico, or you'll drown!" Conner shouted at him. "You can't swim with your leg, and neither of us will be able to carry you across."

Suddenly, they heard a loud roar behind them. Horrified, they looked back to the shore and saw Vexel standing at the water's edge. The hideous beast stood at least twelve feet tall on his hind legs, if not more. His face was half burned with hardly a trace of fur left on his head or neck. There were also noticeable burn patches all over his mammoth body.

The furious beast growled viciously and emitted blood-curdling noises as he stared out on the river at the helpless prey on the raft only fifty feet away. Like a laser beam honed in on its target, his cold, hunger-fueled gaze remained fixed on the defenseless threesome in the water. Then he started toward them.

"Oh my God, he's coming after us!" Jade screamed. "Kick harder, Conner."

When Vexel started to enter the water everyone's fear and adrenaline skyrocketed. Jade and Conner now knew for certain there was no turning back. The only challenge was to get to the other shore as quickly as possible.

Meanwhile, knowing Vexel would most likely pursue the others at any moment, Savi pulled the plastic bag that Luke had given her out of the back pocket of her vest. She moved as fast as she could back up shore and climbed up a rocky incline that led to a lookout point about twenty feet above the river. As she moved along she dropped pieces of the deer's organs after every couple of steps, hoping the smell would lure Vexel away from the river.

"Hey!" she screamed. "I'm up here!"

The hideous creature turned in one direction and then the other, looking for the source of the noise.

"Here I am!" Savi shouted again. "Up here!"

Instantly, Vexel's head swung around and his eyes locked in on Savi standing only a few hundred feet away on the rock ledge.

"Hey!" she screamed once more as she jumped up and down, "Come get me!"

Vexel turned and studied the raft now in the middle of the river. Then he turned back and looked at Savi, still jumping and shouting at him from the rock ledge. Incredibly, he climbed back out of the water and started loping toward her.

"Savi!" Rico shouted. "Jump, he's coming!"

Savi stood near the edge of the rock waiting to ensure Vexel wouldn't return to the water and chase down the others.

"Savi!" Rico wailed.

She waited and watched as her friends floated further away. Then she stared out at the raft one last time and said in a gentle whisper, "I don't hate you, Rico…"

Suddenly, she heard Vexel coming up the hill. He let out a deafening roar when his head appeared from behind the rock.

"Savi!" Rico shouted one last time.

CHAPTER THIRTY-TWO

One look at the size and ferocity of the beast charging at her convinced Savi she couldn't wait any longer. Instantly, she turned and ran as fast as she could over the last part of the rock on which she was standing, pushed off, and plunged twenty feet down into the river. The momentum from her short sprint and final push off of the rock enabled her to hit the water at a 45-degree angle. This saved her from smashing straight into the rocks just a few feet below the water's surface.

Savi was always a good swimmer. But now, just how good, would be put to the test. Upon hitting the water she swam swiftly away and was a good distance from the lookout point before stopping to turn back to determine Vexel's whereabouts. There, she saw Vexel standing up near the place where she had jumped. He roared in protest because his prey had gotten away. Then he quickly disappeared from the lookout point into the nearby woods. Not long after, he emerged from the tree line, charging full speed toward the river.

"Savi! He's coming!" Rico shouted. "Swim!"

By this time, the raft was more than halfway across the river and well above the targeted beach on the other shore. In a desperate attempt to save the boys, Jade now propelled the raft by herself while Conner simply tried to hang on for his life. Though the going was slow, Jade was managing to get them closer to the shore and ultimately to safety. Her tired legs just kept pumping as she held tightly onto Rico's good foot to prevent him from rolling off the raft.

Without hesitation Vexel burst into the water and started paddling in Savi's direction. She was already spent from carrying Rico so far, as well as the hard swim. Gradually, she began to falter.

Conner glanced back and saw Savi struggling in the water, with Vexel in hot pursuit, but he didn't have enough strength to yell a warning.

Savi didn't need a warning. She knew the relentless beast was behind her, gradually closing the gap between them. She dug deeper and continued to swim with all her might. Lifting her head, she spotted the sandbar that Luke had told them about. Realizing she couldn't swim much further without a short break, she made her way toward the sandy island. Before she knew it she had reached the sandbar. Never had touching sand felt so good. Savi crawled on all fours up the sandy mound until the water was behind her. Once her fingers hit dry ground, she collapsed from exhaustion, her face half-buried. For the next couple minutes she laid there fighting for air and trying to regain her strength.

Vexel's hideous looking face bobbed up and down in the water as he paddled slowly but deliberately toward her. When Savi gathered the strength to lift her head again, she locked onto the beast's scarred face coming straight for her. A sense of panic arose within her seeing him less than a hundred feet away.

Unexpectedly, a loud warning siren blared over the area. For a moment, it reminded her of back home and the sound of a tornado warning. Then she realized it was the warning siren Luke had told them about, indicating the dam would open in twenty minutes. It sounded off a second time, and then an eerie silence descended on the river.

Startled by the unfamiliar high-pitched noise of the siren, Vexel stopped paddling for a moment and looked around confused. Once the siren stopped, he refocused his attention on Savi and began paddling hard toward her again. Savi quickly looked over her shoulder and saw that the raft carrying Rico, Jade, and Conner had almost reached the opposite shore. Lying on the sand fully exhausted, she doubted she had the energy to swim the remaining distance. But then she looked again the other way and saw Vexel's ferocious face, now only twenty-five feet away. In one last-ditch effort to save herself she struggled to her feet and stumbled off the sandbar back into the water. Again she swam in the direction of Rico, Jade, and Conner.

"Savi, swim faster! He's catching up!" Rico shouted with all his remaining strength.

No longer able to swim freestyle, Savi flipped over on her back and tried doing the backstroke. Despite her best efforts to elude him, Vexel inched ever closer toward her. Savi knew she was only moments away from being overtaken by the relentless monster. Mustering all her remaining strength, she tried to kick her legs but they no longer moved.

Floating on her back, she watched in horror as Vexel got closer and closer. His heavy breaths filled her ears, together with the sounds of him panting and growling at her. Then a strange peace came over her and she realized after everything they'd been through, she was about to die. Defenseless and out of strength, she floated helplessly in the water waiting for the inevitable to happen. She closed her eyes and said a short prayer, then looked up at the blue sky one last time. Without even the energy to scream, she lay on her back motionless in the water. She closed her eyes once again and hoped the pain wouldn't last too long. Then she whispered one last prayer, "Please God…make it go quickly!"

All of Vexel's hard work had finally paid off. He was now just a few feet from his defenseless prey. Savi floated in the water, calm, still, not wanting to look up at the horrific creature about to kill her. Then a piercing pain shot through her leg as Vexel's claw hooked her ankle. She instinctively recoiled and kicked one last time in an attempt to get away.

Suddenly, the crack of two shots rang out over the river. They came from the lookout point where Savi had jumped in the river just minutes before. Vexel lurched in the water and cried out in pain.

Savi wasn't sure what was happening. She only knew that her ankle was bleeding badly and Vexel was paddling away from her howling in agony. He was making his way back toward the sandbar.

Immediately, Luke dropped his rifle and gear. He dove into the water and began swimming toward Savi. Realizing she was close to drowning, he swam as quickly as he could in her direction. Despite her painful injury, Savi continued to float on her back and do her best to keep her head above water. Vexel, now back on the sandbar, groaned in pain from the gunshot wounds. As Luke swam past the sandbar, he noticed that Vexel was bleeding from both his shoulder and backside. Hearing someone approach the sandbar, Vexel raised his head and gazed at Luke, then growled viciously in his direction.

Again, the siren sounded, this time indicating only ten minutes until the dam was to open.

"Hold on, Savi, I'm coming!" Luke shouted.

Not sure whether she was hearing Luke or just imagining it, she whispered, "Luke?"

"Savi, just keep floating! I'm almost there!" he assured her.

"Luke…is that really you?" she whispered again.

"Hold on, Savi."

Finally, Luke reached the exhausted girl. Her ankle was bleeding badly from the swipe of Vexel's claw, complicating an already difficult situation. She was so weak that she couldn't hold her head up any longer and was starting to swallow water. Luke grabbed her. Then he turned her on her back and put his arm across her chest in a lifeguard hold. Knowing there was no time to spare, he started pulling her through the water toward the shore where the raft had landed.

Exhausted by the swim, along with the added effort of towing Savi, Luke fought hard to get across the river as quickly as possible before the dam opened. He wasn't sure how much time he had, but he knew it couldn't be much. If it opened before they reached shore, they'd be swept down river and, without life jackets on, would surely drown.

"You've got it, Luke!" Rico shouted painfully. "Keep coming."

"Hurry! You're almost out of time!" Jade screamed in a panicked voice.

Luke looked over his shoulder. Only a hundred feet or so lay between him and the shore. Suddenly, the siren rang out again, signaling the one-minute warning before the dam was to open.

Jade and Conner helped Rico to safety away from the river's edge; they propped him up against a pine tree and left him there to watch anxiously as Luke got ever closer to the shore with Savi. After Jade and Conner repositioned Rico safely, they returned to the riverbank.

When Luke saw them standing by the water he yelled, "Move back...or you'll get washed away!"

Immediately, Jade and Conner heeded Luke's warning and hurried away from the riverbank. In a last ditch effort to get to shore, Luke expended every last bit of his strength. He kicked his legs and feet furiously and used the cupped palm of his free hand to pull the water towards him. Suddenly, a series of three short blasts sounded, followed by one long one, indicating the dam had opened. From upriver, a roaring sound cascaded toward them, confirming water was being released into the river.

Despite Luke's warning to stay back, Jade and Conner realized they needed to help him with Savi. Risking their own lives, they darted back to the river's edge and together grabbed Savi by the arms and literally dragged her limp and bleeding body away from the rising current. Meanwhile, Luke crawled on his hands and knees away from the shore fighting to stay ahead of the rapidly rising water. Eventually, he made his way up the bank and out of danger. He flipped over on his back and tried desperately to gasp for air.

Savi's ankle was bleeding and needed attention. Unfortunately, they had no medical supplies with them, and were at a loss as to how to deal with her wound.

"Savi, you made it…You saved our lives," Jade cried, sitting next to her and propping her head up off the ground. Savi didn't have the strength to respond.

Rico, still in a lot of pain, slid his way over to Savi and grabbed her hand. Then he leaned over and kissed her gently on the forehead.

"We made it, Savi. Look, Vexel is about to get swept down the river." Rico pointed at the sandbar that he was standing on.

Savi turned her head and watched as Vexel stood on his hind legs one last time and roared ferociously in their direction. Moments later, the sandbar disappeared under the rising river and Vexel was swept away by the strong current. The last they saw of him he was paddling desperately, and then, he disappeared around the bend of the river.

"Do you think he'll drown?" Jade asked.

"I hope so," Luke said, speaking for the first time since reaching shore. "The current is so powerful right now, I don't see how he could survive. But I'm not going to believe he's dead until I see it with my own eyes."

All at once, they heard the unmistakable swoosh, swoosh, swoosh sounds of propeller blades cutting through the air. Looking up, they saw a small black silhouette against the cobalt blue sky. The longer they stared, the bigger it grew, until it transformed itself into a full-fledged helicopter, the kind that occasionally delivered packages and supplies to Camp Arrowhead.

When the helicopter was in clear sight, Jade began jumping up and down and waving at it furiously. The copter flew right over them as if it didn't see them. Then, it quickly banked to the right and circled back around, confirming it had indeed spotted the group. It hovered a hundred feet above them, its blades stirring up dust and debris on the shore. Moments later, the helicopter's side door slid open and a man with a bullhorn started to speak.

"We see you! We're calling for help! Don't move! We know you have injuries! We are tossing down a medical kit! Help is on the way!"

CHAPTER THIRTY-THREE

The nightmare was finally over. No one could believe what was actually happening. The medical kit was taped closed and tossed out of the helicopter. It slammed to the ground and bounced a few times before settling still. Jade ran over and retrieved it; she peeled the tape away and opened the kit. Savi's ankle was bleeding badly and she was in obvious pain. But she was sitting up and breathing normally. Gradually she started to recover and converse with the others.

Jade cleaned and disinfected Savi's wound, then she bandaged it. The copter had also dropped a few water bottles. Jade gave a bottle to Luke and tried to get Savi to drink, but she declined. After Savi and Luke were tended to, everyone else drank their fill.

The bewildered group sat on the shore. They waited for help and silently marveled at the ordeal they had just survived. Savi was propped up against a rock and Rico against a small tree.

"Luke…you saved me again," Savi said with appreciation beyond words. "I thought I was dead in the water."

"I think they call that a pun," Luke said with a smile. Then he went on to say in a serious tone, "The world needs people like you, Savi…It must not be your time to go."

Savi extended her fingers and touched Luke's hand tenderly, then her face turned serious as well. After a short pause, she turned and addressed the group. "I need to say a few things to each of you without being interrupted…May I do that?" she asked softly.

Everyone nodded and gave their silent permission. Then Savi reached down in front of her and picked up four stones. First, she gave a red-colored stone to Luke.

"Luke, I hope you carry this stone as a symbol of our deep gratitude and enduring friendship. Without you, none of us would be here right now. I will never ever forget you."

Next, Savi handed a grey stone to Conner.

"Conner, may this stone always remind you that you don't have to be anyone else but you. You're a caring person who is funny and brave. And now you've got a couple of cool scars to prove it," she said with a sweet smile.

Then Savi handed a light brown colored stone to Jade.

"Jade, despite the things you've faced in the past, I hope you always know how special you are. And not just because of your beauty, but mostly because of your tender heart. In the end, you were courageous and strong, and played a big part in saving Rico and Conner."

Finally, Savi took the last dark-colored stone from her palm and, with tears streaming down her face, handed it to Rico. As she did she looked at him with great affection and admiration.

"Rico, you're a brave and tender warrior who reminds me a lot of my dad. You're also someone that perseveres through the most difficult circumstances. Someday, when I'm looking for a husband, I want him to be a lot like you…It's too bad you're already taken." Her cheeks turned a deep shade of red as she looked at Jade.

They each sat quietly for a minute thinking about what Savi had said.

Then Luke bent over and picked up a smooth white stone from the ground. But surprisingly, he didn't give it to Savi right away. He just held it in his hand. Then he looked at her tenderly and spoke.

"Savi, since I was a little boy my momma told me to live my life in such a way that I will hear 'seven special words' when I get to heaven.

"What did she mean?" Savi asked in a gentle voice. "What special words?"

He paused a moment and studied her young and tired little face. Then he looked at her straight in the eyes and said, "She meant the 'seven words' I'm about to say to you, Savi."

Then he handed her the white stone he'd been holding, and as he did, he uttered these 'seven words.'

"Well done, my good and faithful servant."

Deeply touched by his words, Savi bowed her head and started to cry.

The tender moment they shared was unexpectedly interrupted when they heard another helicopter approaching. Just behind it, a huge commotion ensued when several vehicles came flying down the access road toward them. The first truck skidded to stop, and a man jumped out of the front and ran straight for them. He had a big bandage on his forehead. As he got closer, he started to look strangely familiar. Then Jade recognized him. Stunned, she couldn't say anything at first. Then she sprang to her feet and practically leapt into his arms. "Doug! You're alive!"

The two of them hugged for the longest time, neither of them daring to let go. When their moment together ended, Doug pulled back and hurried with her over to see Savi, Rico, and Conner.

"I can't believe you're all alive," Doug exclaimed. "We thought you were dead. It's a miracle."

Jade looked over at Doug once again just to make sure she wasn't dreaming all this.

"We thought you were dead as well. How did you survive the rapids after you fell out of the raft?" Jade asked curiously.

He ran his fingers through his hair. "As soon as I hit the cold water, I woke up," he recalled. "Once I came back to my senses and realized what was happening, I rolled over on my back and pointed my feet down river. I rode the rapids about a quarter mile until it slowed, then I swam to shore. A short time later another raft came downstream and rescued me. When the bus got to the pickup point, the driver had a radio and we reported the accident. Rescue teams have been looking for you ever since."

Just then a medical team arrived and began working on Savi, Rico, and Conner. Jade had some bruises and cuts on her arms and legs, but other than that, she was in fairly good shape, especially considering what they had all endured. In the midst of their examination, suddenly the approach of another helicopter filled the air. This one was a rescue copter designed to carry up to six injured passengers.

Once everyone was loaded aboard they were transported back to Camp Arrowhead where a temporary triage center had been set up after the group went missing. Rico was the first into surgery, followed by Savi, and then Conner.

Within a couple of hours they were all lying side by side in the recovery room with Luke, Jade, and Doug hovering over them.

The waiting families were notified that their kids had all been rescued and they were now hurriedly making their way to Camp Arrowhead from the nearby town of Evergreen, where many of them were staying.

Conner's family was first to arrive, followed by Rico's dad, and Savi's parents. The tearful reunion with the thankful families was everything you can imagine. After several introductions, it was obvious Jade's parents were missing. She did her best to fight back the tears as she watched the others welcomed home so warmly.

Then, a huge commotion sounded down the hall, and a woman was yelling excitedly.

"Jade, what's going on?" Savi asked, lifting her head and looking in the direction of the uproar.

Jade shook her head, rolled her eyes, and then responded to Savi's question. "I'm guessing my mother just arrived."

As she had predicted, Jade's mom burst into the room and started looking around, with a frantic expression written across her face. "Where's my, Jade?" she yelled. "Jade!"

"I'm here, Mom," she responded with her inside voice.

"Oh my baby!" her mother cried. "I thought I'd lost you." She bent down and hugged her daughter tightly.

Jade received the hug graciously and returned it. All at once she leaned back away from her mother. She looked her straight in the eyes and said in a deliberate and serious voice, "When we get home, we need to talk."

Instantly, concern registered on her mother's face. "What's going on, Jade? Is there something wrong with you?" her mother asked anxiously.

"Oh no, Mom, on the contrary…There's something very right about me now. It's what's wrong with you that we need to talk about!" Jade said in no uncertain terms.

Just then the medical team insisted the visits come to and end, so everyone could get some rest. Though it took a long time to clear the room, everyone finally agreed to go, leaving Savi, Rico, Jade, Conner, and Luke alone.

Once everyone else had left, Conner was the first to speak.

"I'll miss you guys so much," he confessed. "I really want to stay in touch. After what we've been through, you're more than just friends."

Rico looked over at Conner, shook his head, and smiled. "I can't believe I'm saying this, *hot dog*, but I'd like to stay in touch with you too."

"I'll never forget any of you," Jade admitted. "This was the worst and best experience of my life. Savi, will you call me when you get home?" she asked.

"Sure I will. I was already planning on it," Savi acknowledged.

"Thanks for everything, including the slap," Jade said with a smile on her face and tears in her eyes. "I'll miss you so much."

"You're all always welcome in San Antonio,"Rico offered.

"Same goes for San Francisco," Jade interjected.

"And Chicago," Conner added.

"If you ever want some Southern hospitality? Come see me in Oxford, Mississippi," Savi said, in her own sweet way.

"Well, I guess it's time to say good-bye…again. I'm headed down river to make sure Vexel is dead," Luke told them. "Let's stay in touch. Here's my address at the cabin. We live deep in the woods far away from town. You'll probably laugh but we don't have a phone or computer at the cabin, but I do occasionally check for emails in town. I'll give you that address as well."

"You bet I'll write and email you," Savi promised. "You can count on it."

The others agreed to do the same.

Luke went over and shook hands with Rico and Conner. "You guys should be proud of yourselves. You did good."

After he hugged Jade, he held her hand and looked at her warmly. "You're quite a girl, Jade. You really stepped up at the end and helped save these guys. I wouldn't have thought you had it in you," he said with a wink. "I mean a city girl and all." Jade's eyes again filled with tears as she looked with fondness at Luke and then hugged him for the last time.

"Thanks for everything," she said squeezing his hand as he started to move away.

Then Luke walked over to Savi's bedside and bent down and kissed her gently on the forehead. "Well missy, God must have big plans for you. You should have died more than a few times out there." Tears welled up in his eyes. "My life is better because I met you, Savi…And I don't say that to many people."

Savi and the others couldn't hold back their tears as Luke walked out of the room and disappeared around the corner.

"Do you think we'll ever see him again?" Jade asked Savi.

"I'm not sure," she replied. "But, if I had to guess…I think we will."

ooooo

Well, there you have it. That's how it all went down. I even compared notes with Savi, Rico, Conner, and Luke, to make sure I didn't leave anything out. Even Doug contributed his story. And if you're wondering how I know so much about what happened out in the wilderness…well, that's because I was there. I'm Jade Chang. I arrived at Camp Arrowhead acting like a weak and insecure girl. But I left there feeling like a strong and more confident woman. Rico and, believe it or not, even goofy Conner, taught me many lessons out there in the wild. But it was Savi that changed my life. She modeled faith, hope, and love in ways I'd never seen before. I will always be indebted to her for the impact she had on my life. We all need a friend like Savannah Evans. But don't forget, if you ever meet her...her friends call her Savi.

THE END OF BOOK ONE